ADAM GREEN magazine
issues #1 and #2
+
"the flowers of capitalism"
W0321829

The Flowers of Capitalism

***

Older Brother – Be my manager
Someone as lost as I should not sing
Where's my baby-sitter with her wheelchair?
Where's my leather jacket and ID?

Am I homeless in America without a computer?
A man with a poodle – not a road dog with chops
Without a saxophone
Or a decent street scam …

$$$

Were you expecting to grow, Desert Storm?

While my neighbors in Brooklyn are refreshed by your
skyline

Whether stamp for coin
Or coin of fire

Whether coin of gasoline
Or fire from gasoline

Should I expect flood or omelette?

Gather guitar man, soundman

Thief, and doorman
Guitar-tech and gutter punk (with petroleum mohawk)
Exchange stamps upon the decent streets of Manhattan

Should I expect a million dollars or a nightstick up my
ass?
(Should I expect my skin to transform into leather?)

And my throat filled with cockle
Is it your ears that make that awful noise?
A sober folksinger will save his management

»Subjectivity killed the indie label«

Con Edison is the most tyrannical pimp among us

Waitress in rags ... serving pie to the drunken folksinger
Lesbian corpse buried in a sea of drum loops
Folksinger defiled by Con Edison
His bluesy blood runs undetected through the gutters
of his website
Cleaner than platinum tears from a miracle baby

Pimp of Jerusalem – let us beat them down with our
tomahawks in a blaze of hashish smoke

In the land of Dyckman St.
Where the ice cream gods hold seminars
for the philosophers of Westchester county

Where the Hebrew inscription melts from the matzoh
as dignified as a licorice stain on a sniper's khakis

Where the candied vegetation is slain from the interior

Sluggard of Cyprus

And the limbs of the folksinger dangle from fishing poles
along the banks of the Hudson River (72 leagues
beneath the pigeon's eye)

Picture the vampire bullfrog sucking the prehistoric
tumor on 9th St.

Gawk at the Las Vegas royalty – whose economy is
bonkers …

The jet fuel singes our bullfrog tongues
as bitter as crystal meth without the soul searching

1. »How can we fuck?« she smiles,
squatting on the curbside of our genital junction

2. »I've grown immune to the nighttime magic,« she
smiles,
cogitating the repose of her skanky hard drive

… immune to piggyback rides through traffic

Let Joe Camel negotiate foreign policy – they'll trust
a camel

My love is a slippery red ogre that falls asleep before …

A tour bus is dispatched over London Bridge
Inside the vehicle, we observe the latest Budweiser
simplex

Backstage at the metropolitan café, the replicas cower
under a pale construction of Johnny Depp

Stems and flanks pepper the depot, where the scavengers
poke at the celestial spliff

The scavengers are slippery daredevils – equal parts plant
and animal

At mealtime, we let loose a Bronx cheer for the Skanky
Yankees

I commend the junkie babysitter
when I return home from a long journey
to find my lambs in bed – fast asleep
and none of the china missing

A crusty cigarette burns in the pirate's trembling hand
The stormclouds hang beneath the hulking beanstalk
He thinks that he hears a noise from inside his dressing
room
He makes a pass at one of his seafaring coworkers …
… with devastating results

Desert Storm, I summon you tonight from the archives
of MTV news
May you reappear in Yankee stadium this evening

dressed in Armani with royalty checks in your pockets
Snorting oriental goodies in the lavatory
Protesting the journalistic amnesia that dazzles the
western world

Desert Storm, I will take you on tour with me
My religion will be your soundcheck
I will speak through your crusty cigarette
This crusty cigarette embalmed in skunk blood!

Q: Where is Hussein this morning?
A: Perusing the Magna Carta with cool detachment

Jerusalem, I yearn to roam again in your strip mall
deserts
Wash up on the shore of 79 Tripp St.
and reclaim my kingdom of tangled nintendo cords

I would dwell in the parks
and under the bridges of expired Jerusalem
composing magical paragraphs …

… driving down real roads
holding hands with classmates
feeding ducks (I've fooled ducks all my life)

I've completed my homework assignments scrawled in
the guestbook of the Columbia Hotel

I've combed the meadows of Hyde Park searching for
the key to the mini-bar … on the heels of The Strokes

I've seen the deserts dissolve
and the fruit platters grow larger

I see them overlooking the talents of Kimya Dawson,
    Turner Cody, and Diane Cluck

(Ring Nasan, Rick Shapiro)

A special thanks to Juliet Joslin
from the residents of Mt. Kisco, NY

Completed Aug. 5, 2003

ADAM GREEN

The Civilian

Chorus

1. The roar of the crowds in the cages to the left
2. Ropes of cars tie on by
3. Take your hand and brush the tears from my weeping bible eyes
4. We had a dragon, just to throw things at 'im
5. Wrangle those Johnnies
6. This decision draws light from the river
7. I died unaccomplished and unconscious
8. Wholesome bits of sand lodged their way into my breathing
9. Lady coughing her blood on the beach
10. I also noticed that every good bonus has its »always« quality
11. I'm not going to have a midlife crisis
    (because I had a midchildhood crisis)
12. Use it, don't abuse it, hippies aren't afraid to die!
13. Ricki compliments the king so much that the king eats Ricki
14. The summer comes in and cries
15. Bullfish sat on a rock and fired his secretary
    (»I could get used to this,« he said)
16. New York City's my lint-guard
17. New York comes in like wind
    (and blows my hat off again)
18. *Oh the joy of getting looked at*
    Oh the joy of looking back

Oh the joy of fixing traffic
Build me a twenty sack

19. Strap the pinball to the mutton
20. I was thinking of yellow rectangles when a bomb exploded and threw my cock around the mountain
21. Captain Noodle lived under a bridge
22. Somebody spilled the bagman
23. Cut me off a piece of your sour pie
24. A witchhunt in town separates Captain Noodle from Dixie
25. A historian misreads a political magazine and votes wisely for a different reality
26. A bomb causes lightning to increase in intelligence
27. Springsteen's »pouty lips« photo causes a media splash in the tabloids and lands him a record deal
28. James Brown travels to India
(birth rate goes up .09% per family)
29. Boston crème tampon
30. Murder increases the values of Jeffrey's stocks
31. Jeffrey hires Dixie to paint a fresco on the roof of his vault
32. Universal Sucka (rubber guns)
33. Symptoms taste like cola (love infection)
34. She comes out late when the night is at its darkest
35. Part-time hippy / full-time hooker
36. Cousin love (easy pickins on)
37. A bottle of subway juice
38. Your shoulders are just handles when I fuck you from behind
39. Born to be fine
40. He could pluck me from my bone home

41. Nexterday mornin'
42. In bed with Roger (in bed with an old sick friend)
43. Flinching in front of a wizard's cunt (with the paparazzi all wrapped around)
44. Put on your head rock (Put on your ass clock)
45. A box of cream
46. Neon AIDS (the kool AIDS)
47. Boat music
48. Situational Blues
49. I should get a policeboat and give a hand-job to the ocean
50. Yesterday was Easter and the slot machine just rung
51. And downstairs a shit is delivered to smiling Judy's face
52. Smoke my dreams before the hammers pound them into each other
53. The impossibility of finding good boots confronts two teenagers head-on
54. Crank it endless, forever, for no reason
55. Mee-Haw!!! Mee-Haw!!!

Verse One: Kibbutz

1. Arnid, who lives in a tent outside his mom's house, somehow finds out that he is a member of a lost tribe of Israel
2. Arnid is on a mission from God
(the opposite of balance)
3. People will always be depicted next to animals
4. Can't wait till I'm twenty-one
5. Too many broken hearts in my head

Verse Two:
We made your mind to offend us

1. We created your mind to offend us
2. My format has gone bad
3. I wanna throw away my piece of pie
4. The phone is at the door
   (a car wearing expensive clothes)
5. Holes between the pages

Verse Three:
When the dustballs settle in the morning

1. The wax retractor (a gun named son)
2. We dance through a maze of a million awkward days
3. Little dead bird lying hideous and still
4. The disease that you became
   (where everything seems so insincere)
5. Breathe in birds and spit out bones
6. Kissing your face (my favorite project)
7. Show me an orphan and I'll show you a computer
   that cries

Verse Four:
You've got holes in your pants,
but they look good

1. Hey Animal Hands!!
2. Do I have what it takes to be exposed?
3. How could we have realized that we'd died?
   (Lord, nobody took us aside)

4. It's brand-new everything!!
5. In a world where nothing's really true
   (what's a trusting guy like me to do?)
6. Dad was there in uniform
7. Oh Baby, I want to sell you on something beautiful

Verse Five: We were hard

1. We had a dragon, just to throw things at 'im
2. A squirrel ran by, I know what he's thinking
   (I am O.K. as the world)
3. You want to fuck your teachers
4. Mario can fly!! (I put on my happy pack)
5. We don't need to look up to thank God anymore
6. I left my drug box under the stripping pole

Verse Six: Everything happens intuitively

1. The future smells like burning teeth
2. My bird against your nest
3. Lost in the garden of princely pleasures
4. »We'll take it!« (The real deal)
5. Surrender your body to the present tense
   (Surrender your bed)
6. Even grape juice has needs
7. I never want to have a body again
   (they'll never let you stop pushing the boulder)
8. Microchips in their feces
9. Everyone in groups of three
   (thinking god is only theirs to see)
10. A bunch of actors at a crying convention

11. The tide is rising in your bedroom
12. Follow you into your bedroom store
13. I thought everything was free
    (until I found myself in jail)
14. Value is beautiful
15. The rapes were so malicious
    (but the chex-mix was delicious)
16. Adam Green
17. I'm going to give my shoes away, I hope I don't want
    them back

Verse Seven:
I only feel comfortable dressed like an asshole

1. Feeling like a drag queen (feeling like an in-between)
2. Nestled inside carpets of bad breath
   (pissing hot ones)
3. Errors of the tongue (whose lisping makes me come)
4. Crawling out of crotch (cherries in underpants)
5. You are what you don't want to hear
6. Even if I could be anywhere
   (I would still have to be there)
7. I was born, I cried (I lived a life, I died)
8. Adam Green appreciates others
   (I look so great reflected in your eyes)
9. Who's counting?

Verse Eight: Pokemon chewable Ritalin

1. Pokemon chewable Ritalin
2. The chair was huge like a building

3. Inside the taxidermist's secret workshop
(there's a billionaire stuffed with dirty socks)
4. I told the story of my life then tripped and fell down on a knife
5. I'm looking down the tunnel at her and she's waving back
6. Shoot your face to death (some »real faced« dead guy)
7. Thank you for delivering this fungus to my feet
8. How far can I bend my love
(and know she'll kiss me back?)
9. I want to tear up other organisms (hairy plastic)
10. I need to put this piece of shit behind the monkey statue
11. Leather sky, made of sky (Leather rain, made of rain)
12. Play some time games (maybe play some time-bomb)
13. Information is a smelly brown creation
14. Red bricks drop from your vagina
15. *Carolina (she's from Texas)*
Her lips taste like sunk ships
(her breasts taste like breakfast)
16. She could suck me through the payphone
17. You can't trick the ground

Verse Nine: I can't work

1. Talk is cheap (but that's all I'm selling)
2. I camped out in the elevator
3. You can lean right through them
(You can fuck yourself to them)
4. Tell me did you listen to his song?
(Was it so good that you had to masturbate along?)

5. I wanna ride a horse with crutches
6. They're backing you into the corner where they feed you
7. I bring all the menus to the pigsties
(I laugh for the wood when the axe dies)
8. Riddled with guilt (griddled with milk)
9. I carefully open the door for each new kiss to come through
10. Let's start by finishing
11. He wouldn't talk for 1000 days

Verse Ten: I got a glimpse of the new you

1. We exited the bathhouse
(don't build your house in the hallway)
2. All punishments are pieces of dying
(I was always her favorite patient)
3. You are a free walker
(You are making them suck on your tongue)
4. I saw the dead child in the pond (and it's us)
5. I took one of her curly red hairs
(and put it in with my own)
6. Machinery of the night
7. Press play and turn this party on
8. Business is booming (but Moneybags lives alone)
9. Smoking cigarettes for the good guys

Bridge

1. New York City wore its bridal gown
2. The garden is milking a child
(under the green lightbulb)

3. Mountains of wine swim beneath the watery sheets
4. Wire frames of jagged nipples suspended by strings of wind
5. Songs of slight experience
   (a computer was my Christopher C.)
6. Times Square was my hemlock tree
7. All of my pages are open at once
   (bright lights on old skin)
8. I went to the hospital (to have a good think)
9. Blind as I was mortal (I fell towards the light)
10. If I was going to fuck a little boy without knowing it
    (by mistake), this is how I would do it:
    a) masturbate constantly
    b) forget my dreams
11. Mirror in the haystack
12. I masturbated so much that my right hand left me.
    (So then I started using my left hand. And my left hand *right me*!)
13. I lie back like a sultan
    (and watch your blue shadow perform)
14. I don't expect to be jerking off ever again
15. I knew a farmer who used to beat his kids
    (to water his corn with their tears)

Verse Eleven: Bread in bed

1. Things I need tomorrow: job, soap, towel, blanket, cup, lightswitch, front door
2. Help me Papa, Mama don't like it when I play in her underwear
3. New York is married but she still wants one last kiss

4. I forgot that I loved you 59 times this minute
5. Run down to 1st Street and play a G-chord
(Then run down to 2nd Street and play a C-chord)
6. The cowboys were seduced by the indians there
7. Stealing Pandora's cigarettes
8. *We met John at the boat show*
(with arrows pointing at him)
He told us a number
(to Woodstock we did follow)
9. We need healthy soldiers to trace on fleshy canvas
(the box of human salad)
10. Tossing Heaven's salad

Verse Twelve:
I love you on my own

1. Wrangle those Trudys and Judys and Moes
(Wrangle those Johnnies all the way home)
2. She wrangled those Johnnies through a hallway beneath her home
3. Who slipped a roofoo in my gingeroo?
4. Wrangle those rainbows
5. Bones in the pudding (children in the chowder)
6. More like an artist is less like a lady
7. Dixie came to New York to become a famous rave dancer
8. The triumphs of maggots (sprinkles of tarantulas)
9. The ground is anything that the rich don't have to touch
10. Tumble of love

Verse Thirteen:
She's an old crow

1. A green nylon lobster
2. I spray my geometry
3. Gun buddies
4. I have a limp in my cosmic shuffle
5. No.K.

Verse Fourteen:
Sunny days in the butcher's office

1. Raspberry wooden cunts (sandpaper kokomo)
2. Green felt vagina
3. My big bulbous fingers breaking all my little friends

Verse Fifteen:
I met Chad at the Phish show

1. Reaching blind into the deepest mouth
   (in the brownest part of town)
2. The beggar's hand: a bottomless hole
   (strap a sidecar to my left foot)

Bonus Verse:
Tickling the bronze statue

1. My life as someone who fucked Kathy who had AIDS
2. Every day I escape in-between the golden bars

Verse Sixteen:
Tape a horseleg to my painting

1. I just robbed a liquor store earlier today
2. Animals come out like spokes on his crown
3. Spill the beans until they break
4. Masturbation – my own civil war
   (while you tiptoe around my indian)
5. The ash between my toes
6. I met the king (and he autographed my wings)
7. We sputter through the maze of night
   (only to greet morning's mocking light)
8. (cup, cup)
9. In bed with a raisin (In bed with an old sick friend)
10. My drum machine gun flute
11. The patchy-haired beauty
12. Just let my tired fingers wander upon her body's
    golden stages
13. I shot my road
    (when now is now is now is now is now)
14. Pink highways (tea and traffic)
15. Build a mouth faultlessly (cross a street angrily)
16. Build your own vagina
    (think of a new beer can design)
17. Ride the carrots down the hill
    (running from the neon lobster)
18. Britney Spears came down from Heaven and drew
    a line in the sand
19. My bones clicking against the refined scrambled fuzz
20. Eyes which tickle armies bright
21. I press down against her sword

22. Stuck my dick into a revolver
(thank god it went click)

Verse Seventeen:
Stuck in front of the mirror

1. My condemned future aspires, realizing itself to be homeless as it converges
2. Fab was mad at his friends for not letting him protect them (so he hurt himself)
3. If death comes as a carpenter
(I want to have sex with time)
4. The intestines of a beetle taste like strawberries.
(The intestines of a horse taste like peanut butter)
5. *Like a broken clock laughing at an empty drug box*
Like a duck-fucker reaching for a sack of duck cocks
6. You'll never be as black as me
7. The king's on drugs (goodnight to the light)
8. Sinking to the bottom of his song
9. The king is kissing spiders
10. She's ripping the stairway off of her vagina
11. I kidnapped this cool kid
12. Trading me broken clocks for stolen pictures of superman
13. I untie my dick from yours
14. Britney Spears came down from Heaven and choked a cobra with her muscular thighs
15. Penis fever
16. Free-airline-movie joy
(earning-money-in-a-swimming-pool joy)
17. There is a dick all over my homeless ass

18. Think about all the sex I could have been having while she was cheating on me
19. I want to know the truth about having sex with men
20. These children taste like monsters

Verse Eighteen:
On my way to sexual doom

1. How many genital outlaws in this room?
2. Sharp red clowns raining from the horny sky
3. Sticking their dicks in the spike-filled bags
4. She had a hot racist body
5. The improvements being made on the passengers
6. American castle – the lips of the house door (the chimney farts)
7. Honey on the wires
8. Annie takes the skin of the sea and carries it behind her like a towel
9. Butterfly beaks (riding the trainbow to Dreamland)
10. I got to go play for the Yankees (but I can't find my way to the field)
11. I swear by the government that I love you
12. Pooping jellyfish
13. Corporate recommended fate
14. My mother guided my father into me
15. Row, row, the subway car (through the Russian fields)
16. Trouble flashed its bush at last and left me in disguise
17. The beast in me (has found a place in society)
18. She has my pussy (deep in the heart of the shopping mall)

19. Her mouth was too big to blow me
    (so she wiped my ass instead)
20. Camouflaging the sex act
21. What am I doing in New York City?

Completed Sept. 11, 2001

Verse 12, Line 7 Concept by Jest Commons
Verse 17, Line 2 Written by Kimya Dawson
Verse 17, Line 6 Written by Emil Africa
Captain Noodle is a character created by Jest Commons

ADAM GREEN
magazine
ssue
2

Frozen Gay Turtle

The songs I used to get used to Jesus
Abomination of the first world order – a pearl is lifted
from a blue shed – taken to the sizeable emperor, and
disposed down the inside of a country
My sister – the legend
The legend of order
Memory of the joggers of Tripp St.
Germans dispose of the joggers of Tripp St.
The animal has arrived at JCPenney
Ancient sexuality
The wrinkled doorways collide in the most wretched
mission
The clicking insect hands
(where the tennis balls exist on fiery pedestals)
Burn the Germans but remember to tell us why you
chose to
A while of time from before – she caught one of those
plant diseases
Nazi whalers
An example of computer language:
Bless this Jewish computer
Jesus was a Rockefeller
To Nixon – who ended up selling merch to all the
playa-haters
The ninja dicks I sold had skill mothafucka
Mothafucka hate cha motha
Send this dick to college
To Nixon – who ended up writing a song for every *dick*
in college

The terrifying leap from one human to another
Just like the ninja became my best old friend while my
body was in college
I have arranged my family in a way that most people
could never find adequate
Mother cannot see inside my wilderness
Where their breasts float like painted ships upon a harbor
of thigh
Perhaps a little taste of the harbor
Perhaps another juice in the tower
Perhaps another boy for dinner
I wonder if his beard was taller than his wit
A trinket from God is what swings from everyone's
brain
A woman is a hospital
Jealous of every woman I see
William was without odds in every scene
Joey – you run to me bro – with your post-coitus album
for them all to see
I think I heard the girls badmouthing him at the
breakfast eating Olympics
All artists work in caricature
The technique of the smooth tongue
Oh, how the mouth waters for want of more mouth
All songwriters are gay to some extent
List of complexes:
I want to have sexual experiences with all the people
I know
(even if they're only combing the hair of the whiz kid
that's touching me)
Does one chase after his second mother for sex?

This is one of the toughest brainskins I've ever seen cut
all the way through
So don't tell us you've been hiding all of your piss
between the blankets
Jameson liquor disclosed – the porn star lives
with three fans
Quiz time – Whose sex justifies our own life?
German sex story – the blonde gave the cuban a bite
Other Music – a store with great vision
And Kim's also a remarkably visionary store
The swollen keys of a tattered laptop
Chasteball – the game that a celibate man plays
Problems the two of us encounter: keeping the story
straight
Rapidly re-piecing the past, and feeding it to the howling
mouths
One of us was leaning against the wooden farm fence –
»That's great shit man, classic shit.«
(as man moves into hello)
I don't want to die, right?
Give me some kind of demands
Gimme some storkies, I need more storkies!
To him I am my brother
The crumpling paper towers
Here is my phone number, come over and sex me up
The crumpling paper trousers of a child-pornographer
Every victim in town needs a copy
A nose wiggles in the ass
My bed is falling off my bed
The writing on the toes
The times her mercy shows

Again until forever
To my parents – I inherited every piece of your cowardice
Fashion plugs
Ghosts in the couch cushions
I would never really murder someone, I wouldn't want to deal with the mess
Can a government be lovers?
Mr. Bootlegger spends the winter in jail
The roar of the crowds is him singing in jail
The new Manhattan
The book of dead slackers
Levi's punk rock jeans with new neon zipper rockpockets!
The new TV sitcom boy@house is one of the most fundamental courses in your child's emotional education
Play idea:
A boy is doing badly at Michael Jordan University. For his birthday, his dad buys him »The Book of Dead Slackers«
He is dead in the way that nobody needs him
We need to borrow your jeans for the punk rock exhibit
Some security guards are searching a man, »Please stop searching me!« he exclaims.
I'm going to lick the tits off that sticky pop
The Poo Poo Plopper shop
Lobsters are far more popular for humans to eat than guinea pigs
In twenty years, insect meat is going to be more widely used in comedy than
both SPAM and chicken combined!

Because there is more food out there than in stomachs
Things don't suck anymore ... they fuck!
This sandwich fucks
Can the fuck-drenched government suck a piece of metal
through a glistening urethra?
Arthur stared at the negress as she shit on the airplane
seat
This airplane food fucks
This airplane fucks!

(*)

An airplane between the cotton sheets – – –

(*)

Government is a dick word
The most important story ever forgotten
I was sticking my dick in her cookie as her stuffing
fell out
Adam and Kimya fuckpics
For my life what would I like to have?
»Who's on the screen bitch?!?!«
I can make friends
Government fucks
Hitler's downfall was that he believed the speeches
that he made
I can't care for the cure
I am scared of getting beaten up, obviously
Break a myth
One of the reasons why I will eventually move away
I step inside the alligator
Gonna buy you a brand new busboy

Gonna steer you down the stairs
What's the brand of your boat?
Coffins that say »Oh no!« on them
Things fall down in the dark
Steven Jesse Bernstein had a major influence on my life
»There is a certain poetry in comedy« (There is a certain comedy in cactuses)
I only can watch those tapes
They are only inside jokes because the outside isn't familiar with them, isn't that true Roger?
Inside joke videos
When we understand enough about the system to ride it
You would hope that people who get married are co-dependent instead of just plain dead
Stare into your internal nigger
I need to check my e-mail to see if Bruce Springsteen wrote me back
The word »care« means six different things
Give me an inch of money
Money-plated horses (Cigarette-plated sailors)
The echo of my mother's flesh
The drugs of the deadly past
The ceiling fan begins to bubble
I am like how she used to feel like
»I lied to the doctor. I told him I didn't smoke pot«
Dennis denies the mistake (I deny the date)
Everyone was tapping on my back as I kissed her with my eyes closed
Touched by a town
J-Lo's infinite wisdom
Always looking towards the camera together

Everyone whose soul is being sucked up by the camera
ought to retaliate and get a camera of their own
Let's get a camera and kill these fucks!
And so everyone's world is being sucked out of them
I'll suck your world out of you
It's time to get a camera of our own
As the tent slips down and the rags become our homes
And the boat sails down into the muddy ground
Just as a child has an emotional effect on its teacher, a bad
consumer has an emotional effect on Winona Ryder
Trapped in a venereal disease fortress
Their pants fell down and they reattached their sex
backwards
Nowadays the focus is more on the individual (bullshit!)
A stage squirrel
Teenage mutant ninja squirrels
Diff'rent squirrels, for diff'rent turtles
Top 10 worst moments of the year:
1. Getting lynched in a turtleneck at a Pop Art funeral
2. Finding the gay turtle frozen inside a block of ice at the
top of Mt. Olympus
So often do I visit my pirate friends, that they rarely
realize that I'm gone
»Frozen Gay Turtle« is such a Hermes rip-off!
My goal seems to be to change her and then to discard
her
Eyes that ask for more armies on their bright television
screens
I'm going to write the equivalent of »On the Road« for
my generation. It's going to be called »Stay at Home«
Las Vegas Pinstripes

The shoe maniac molests slipper in Vegas!
Looking towards your call
Looking towards a time when a wrong mouse-click will result in a bad smell
»Lincoln paid Wilkes Booth to murder him because he was ashamed of their gay love affair and did not want to continue to live as the only gay president that there ever was!«
I appreciate the hematology here
The goddess of twin soldiers
Her fingers are fantastic
The wind shall blow sarcastic
Her tongue is like a brush
My dick is sore from trying to fuck those stegosaurus bones
The freedom of the infected
The trousers collapsed on the carpet
By being doctors they became lovers to their patients
(We all need a camera, etc ...)
The servitude of happiness
My body should be able to withstand three farts without scattering in lonely paths
My body scolds itself – for the want of control
My body is a comedy (a skeleton of a ninja priest)
My soul is farts
Ninja Jesus (Disease him in his skytop diner with his ninja toast and birds)
Girls are just boys with vaginas
I fly back to the girls on a wave of retarded Asian sound
The deep dark family secret
The reflexes of reason
(a teardrop falls on a backpack filled with rubble)

How many rooms in your pocket?
Burning a picture of paste
She'll just fly across the river until a bridge runs through her
»Oh How I Miss This Toe So« by Dr. Seuss
There's been nothing left to say since she showed me those videos
Insect penis trading cards
The tanned in a world of white
(married to the stolen sky)
Hunger fucks you as it eats you
Punch her vagina till she believes in college
Just because you shouldn't be jealous doesn't mean that she's not amazing

A phone interview with the folksinger:

Sing Out!: Where are you right now?
Folksinger: I'm in a dusty room. I'm tripping on acid, Jim.
Sing Out!: How would you describe your music?
Folksinger: People don't understand how mathematical it is. How math applies to my music. As with all sciences, the discarded becomes the gold. I think they would be good songs to sing in jail.
Sing Out!: So you work hard on the songs?
Folksinger: Wow, you really pulled that boner out of its coffin.
Sing Out!: I don't understand.
Folksinger: I'm like a musical Nazi. Not people … music. I'm an uncompromising artist.
Sing Out!: What are your musical influences?
Folksinger: I think people should start to appreciate

math a little more. People don't realize that Satan is an angel too.
Sing Out!: What are your future plans?
Folksinger: I don't know. I have to go, it's time for my date.
There's an ogre that lives in the mall (and he hates little girls)
Bombs in Central Park (wheelchairs pushed by the sun)
Please don't adjust that dial (because this radio has feelings)
Vintage boys are growing beards
»One of my major influences was Nickelodeon«
Never caught a nicer trap (it sounds like your ears)
Rehearse your mornings
Deep-fried mantra (The sandals thicken around the statue's toes)
Franchises germinate   Germs apologize   Crystal replicas
Cold gas and brass blood   Inexplicably nubile
Lovelorn running in a rainstorm   Ghosts of Africa
Factions facing off   Feathery dreadlocks
Refugees scrubbed clean   Primitive silkscreen
Fetal politics   A heart-wrenching retard
Diplomatic crush   Jilted iron lungs   Kiss me, copycat
Rape me secretly   Geriatric curse   Miniseries dads
Frozen restaurant   Laser apple laugh   Heavenly fish tails
Body locks   In the ghetto of this house
Swollen rubber henchmen   Gabardine hex
Rocky Mountain jam   Western galaxies
Geranium horsepower   Indulging stale lingo
Hedonistic musk
25-cent hospital   Night-walker's paradise
Open-air parade

Marooned in paradise   Hijack the parade
The master of the drugs   Poison needle smoker
Pulsating oracle   Squadron of cosmonauts
Fetal astronauts   Smoking frozen nectar
Drowning in a bag of nerve gas   Freshwater dungeon
Nuclear priestess   Prize-winning dungeon
Riding a Florida three blocks back   Packinghouse fight
Oxygen coupon   Rocking horse of love   American kiss
My brother – the prophet   Penny chicken
Autistic hooker   Creamy English mouth
Soupy framework
Looking for a deeper soul to detonate
Discarding countries
Droning rocketships   Luscious rumours
Crank the carnival
Leather sanctum   Electric mobster   Perfect dummy
Landfill baby   Starfish spaghetti   Styrofoam pillars
Siamese crab boy   Neolithic curse
Safety in the middle of a pay-zone
A marriage that extends beyond the approval of friends
»My coat's more full of holes than a Pittsburgh infield«
In between prizes
An anorexic cherub
A hand from the forest reached inside the taxi
Bagelheart (reclaim the flood)
A piece of that door is still in my heart
Friend to admirer (person to animal)
An educated dream (the toasted moment)
My bed is a platter
The angel awoke with soap in his wings
I've been away at war (at the bookstore)
With my eyes pressed against the bookshelf

And the silver-faced Chinaman looming behind
A torn garment draped over the Magna Carta
Behind me, a Roman telephone is swollen
Animal hands grasping for the oars (furry fingers
    hesitating)
Stems of basketballs (the instruction manual to the mall)
An insect heart is booming from the center of
    every microphone
The oars are powered by electric barnacles
I dined with the silver-faced thug tonight
    (he consumed the majority of the beetle corpse)
Every parent sent their child down the river and at the
    delta they were sorted
Bread in chains
Every store is a suspect (every storefront is constipated)
Slowly, I began to fall in love with my gun
View from beneath a funeral
Last time I was quizzed, I couldn't remember the colors
    of the UN flag
Ever since I've been walking around with a broken
    joystick, I've gone into emergency life mode
Emergency fantasy (terminal forecast)
»I'm not that good, but I'm extremely OK«
Square cats   Psychic flowers   Jackie Noff
Emotional stuntman
»There's nothing like sliding down the back of a giant
    friend«
Playing chess with my soul (or no soul has me)
Neurology is more important to me than songwriting
    (I dabble in sex)
Frozen Gay Turtle: the Bob Dylan story

Appendix:

I'm at the end of my wood
Look at him go through the women, not saving an eye for any man
Two men embrace in the doorway of their country home
The fourth skin of night (the moon has gone to college)
Oh how I roamed from couch to couch (oh how I stumbled from moon to moon)
These girls like to get down slow (superior blues)
The United Sacks of Fear
Don't shit on my sunshine (with your fuck-ugly face)
I sang so I would not feel the terror (Helen Keller on acid)
»I don't know enough about the Chinese to call you a racist«
The wind is the soul of the planet
Outside the hotel the van is getting packed
Hardcore disease channel
Kissing holes in the airplane wings
With a rock critic holding my hand, I take a tour of my homeland
»I'm allergic to handshakes« (I want to kill the soft soul)
Wet towel in a freezer   Aluminum moustaches
Toilet paper cigarettes
An orgy of light (a century of doubt)
Foreign guys have the biggest cocks (blue jokes)
Party in my backpack – It's a book about a blowjob that became a lifestyle
»I caught a nose in the voicestream«
Cowboy sauce
The dead girl cries at the bottom of the envelope (her royal queef)

Blood punching holes through blood
Faded top-ten list in a dusty hall of fame
Went to a brothel right before my show
    (but the hooker jerked me off too slow)
The joy of knowing someone in common
»People who want to kiss your shit before you flush it«
Summertime bruises (I shiver with an orgasm of fear)
The interiors of pain
I can hear you applying yourself in the other room
A particular brand of Native-American humor
Starsick (the pope shit the throne)
Negotiate with the disease

Completed Dec. 24, 2002

CHAPTER IV.
* * * * * * *
8 PAGES FOR ALLAH

8 pages for Allah

*** Part 1 ***

Google Search: Farmer Dave
Search results (ranked 10-20)
10. Farmer Dave: Celebrity profile – a premium creation from the foul peoples at Magical America LLC
11. »It's one of the earliest dreams I can remember,« cites Dave, »I'm at McDonald's with my lover …«

In between shower fucks, we caught up with Farmer Dave at his Geneva parish.
> Google Search: Bagelheart

Deep in the heart of the Jewish wilderness …

The war drums are pounding as Chief Bagelheart begins his sermon
Beat hard the drums of equality
Tee-pees detonate behind the shaman … wampum sprays out like popcorn

Once upon a failed marriage
A screaming fan jumped onstage
In a flash, she grabbed the dying child
And retreated to Israel

We are REAL INDIANS from the woods
More indigenous than our cousins the trees
Smarter than the sun and earth combined

BACK, BACK > username: Farmerdave@juno.com
password: js##injunjoe6y6*l2o

Staring into the eyes of some yankee dream
Farmer Dave scoots by the skyscraper
Ms. President follows shortly, tripping over various porn links
Before descending the subway stairs

Later that evening ...
Ms. President is adjusting the interface on her bedside mantel
She rubs the corporate insignia and sighs
A nightmare smile slowly rises within the portal of her mouth

While Ms. President sleeps
The engines of terror flex beneath the Arabian sky

Monday June 22, 2004
Farmer Dave is in transit ... we receive queries from his mobile office
C:\TERRORISM\anthrax.doc

On your average day
Farmer Dave lives in a hairy house with jelly walls
Where a telepathic drone drips from the anal tap

A doctor's hand twisting in the hallway frightens Dave
(We are much larger than Dave)

Google Search: Magical America Bagelheart
Search results (ranked 1-10)
3. Magical America LLC introduces a Bagelheart Plug-in

*** Part 2 ***

Chief Bagelheart slouches between his two wives (sisters)
He is of medium height, broad-shouldered and deep chested
A bagel-necklace strung across his tits
He speaks frankly with his doctor

Ms. President enters the wigwam at the side door
Bagelheart rolls by in a hospital bed
Farmer Dave peers out from his rectum across the operating table
Dr. America performs the scalp dance

Hey Mister, do you mind if I try on your backpack?
Google Search: Ms. President naked
Results (5-10)
7. Ms. President fuckpics – sailor bones swirling in the harbor
Pic 1, Pic 2, Pic 3, Pic 4, etc…
8. Bagelheart family tree – Ms. President > Begat Jew President > Begat Nigger Woman, etc…

I turn to the good Chief and ask what ails him
»Prostatitis,« he replies, »I have a small potato where my prostate should be.«

He speaks frankly with me
»My hands were the first to go ...«
»The good news,« he chuckles, »is that I'm going to die.«

Thursday, June 24
Next morning I send out 3 anthrax letters
I begin to regard bio-terrorism as an act of purification
(Like all men, I'm a bit of a Jackson Pollock in bed)

»Two-cent reward for the capture and return of
  Farmer Dave«

The gifted doctor lives at an urban address
Alongside vomiters and three-headed billionaires
Down on the street, a mound of warriors fossilize
A cowardly terrorist done slashed their limbs

Three blocks east ...
Roman sentries chase after frolicking farm girls
  in the park
Whilst bisexual tourists stroll beneath a canopy of
  totem poles
I follow them down to the Grand Canal and marry them

Mom and I drive to my tuba lesson
Ms. President teaches tuba in her garage
(which is filled with all kinds of junk)

I'm at my tuba lesson now
Michael Jackson asks if he can try on my backpack ...
  absolutely!

He says that he is going to bury a treasure chest
filled with his own gold records ... *can I help to dig*
the ditch?

Michael Jordan wears Hanes
But what kind of drawers does Jacko wear these days?
(Ms. President seems distracted though)

Farmer Dave was a lesser-known college basketball coach
Before he got caught taking bribes in Michael Jordan's
trophy closet
He spanked me in front of Michael J. Fox

How would YOU feel if the King of Pop just crumbled?
I used to look up to that guy ... I'm so ashamed
For the first time in my life, I have contemplated suicide

*** Part 3 ***

There is a ragged package from Farmer Dave
It is still on the mantel along with last year's letters and
numbers
(I can't bear to open it)
All thoughts turn to my lamb ...
She would be annoyed if she saw me and Ms. President
together
She is a perfect American

I see Bagelheart wading through internet vistas
Swiping ocean waves through military code-readers
He reaches for the sun buck-naked and exposed
Why should it be that rich kids pay him to self-castrate?

Adam Green Magazine: Issue #4c
1. Saddam Hussein: Hollywood Dictator
My hand upon his sneakers worn
My heart deplore his trousers torn
2. An erotic mini-moment:
Stumbling through the walls of night
I fell before a cave of light

Snug within Bagelheart's tanned caboose
Farmer Dave mingles with bacteria
»There's enough jism in here to concoct a makeshift venereal disease«
There is a new region!

Ms. President comes to me with a big problem …
I wiggle my forceps and peer into the maze of her vagina
Within seconds, I uncover a well of unmarked tears
And the diamonds of St. Thomas
And a young Farmer Dave

Bridge:

1. Yellow reeds as side doors on the merry blue indian wheel
2. That night, I dreamed that Mike Tyson wanted to fuck me
3. The next morning, I figured out how to write bubble letters
4. I felt special, and entitled to my own sensitivity
5. He has broken down a barrier between himself and his tape recorder
6. Searching desperately for a suitable distraction

7. A man needs a calendar to masturbate on schedule
8. Computer game interface …
   (videogame cartridge guts)
9. Smell of erasers and dried saliva on dick
10. »You can't suck on negative space«
11. *Snake eyes red dots like skittles*
12. Animals are the most precious jewels
13. I wasn't exactly raving about the kindness in her eyes
14. Wooden sandwiches (vaginas)
15. I agree with about 50% of your blurbs
16. My backpack is the portal
17. »Women are basically great … until they start to
   move«
18. »People are basically good … unless I'm cold«

Now inside of the giant golf ball at Disney World …

Michael Jackson and I have decided to eat at Kellogg's
Diner
Tonight, the booths are candy-apple red
The tunnel of love is a passageway through Michael
Jackson's eyes
She doesn't want for her love to look like mine

I present George Lucas as the Wizard of Oz
He lurks behind a curtain composed of the fabric of
entertainment
Escaped prisoners dig ditches in the lemon sunset
Their empty pockets wet with hot human gore

Broken sick disease

Cut into pieces and rolled down the hill
But the sickness continues to express itself regardless

Jew President pulls up alongside us in a fancy wagon
Chief Bagelheart and Ms. President climb aboard the wagon
And return to camp

*** Part 4 ***

Dr. America just sits and stares
»We don't usually associate pain with this sort of thing ...«
I saw the gold bars rising from behind the mountain
I bind my love in skunk blood

Last year we tamed a wild hooker
And completed a comprehensive study on heroism
This year, we pose as an Egyptian rock star
At the Times Square Exhibit

Bagelheart, as diseased as his mannerisms will indicate
Crouches behind the sidewalk vendor, fingering his bagel necklace
Detectives scan for escaped prisoners amongst the rubble
Glitter, vagrants, insipid lies!
In the meantime, I suggest that you make up with your ex-boyfriend
I love his Mt. Kisco accent

The dust of rainbows hails down on 9th St.

A buzzing noise fills the bathroom
Hair clippings collect on the tile floor

Dr. America is leafing through his stamp collection
In-between clients, Ms. President heats a pot of peasant
soup
I know that sound ... it's the sound of anticipation
She'll be home soon with my wedding present

Bagelheart lies supine on the operating table
Bungee cords lodged in his gamey throat, tears streaming
down his face
A pale orgasm brewing in his gut
I peel him from the train-tracks and plant him in my own
private garden

I'm trying to maintain a smile while my car is in the shop
Allah, let the waves of emotion guide these words
into melodies
Peasant girl!
Who birthed a litter of colored miracles!
Who was trained in intellectual discourse!
Who bleeds with tenderness upon my empty socket soul!
A recovering negro!
It's like being the captain of a ship that never reaches land
And we try to forget the meaning of the sport

She insists upon a rigid heritage
Ashamed of slavery
And all those who tested positive for obscenity
Ms. President chucks a spear in my direction

So embarrassed by injustice!
Such hysterical crying!
She clamps my head in place …
To see the rich boy smiling
While my father is crucified beneath the table
I flee with child to the shrine of Hollywood

Ashamed of guestlists and testicles
Embarrassed by tenderness and shame
Ashamed of words and diseases
Ashamed of embarrassment and the trappings of
sickness …

Spears rain down on 9th St.
Impaling the sacred hippies of Manhattan
Energy spills into the ground

Where are the majestic gods of limitless magical
freedom?
Question: Where have all the ladies gone?
Answer: Cursing and working for tips
The fluffer grabs my cock and tugs

Rejoicing in the music of his holy heart-song
Farmer Dave drives a spear into Ms. President
Beat hard the drums of circumstance
The spectrum of judgement is obscured by dreams of
reward

We ride on the mandibles of a nuclear cyclops
Our body is a fractal society

Betrayed by a tremendous wave of energy
Our subway prayers subverted by black magicians
Ms. President, you should turn yourself in

The hand inside the camera now forms an angry fist
Betrayed by empty pleasures and false coupling!
Betrayed by nerve damage and hopeless light!

Bluebirds shaken mad in a purple tornado
Murdered at the waist and coughing up clay
We pray for swooping angel arms to extract us
We pray for the hand outside the machine …

*** Part 5 ***

Cut my friend, Tell no lie
See me tell my friend is spy

It's 1986
I am 5 years old – it's the first day of kindergarten
Jesse Tisch sits beside me building with blocks
We are trying to construct the Eiffel Tower
(Back then, I rarely appreciated constructive criticism)
Shhh…the dog crucifix is sleeping
Crab crawls up leg reaching for pubic sun
The expression of personal preference is our sport

Take my wife for example
A perfectly disciplined broad
She comes home every night (give or take a few)
And always massages my broadside before bedtime …

Splintered wooden secrets lurk inside the bubbles
Coral bands capsize through the laser code-reading
machines
Note: It takes a code-reader to disrobe a game
And to reveal the machinery underneath
Whoever sells the game gets the most money and the *first*
laugh

I carry with me a hemisphere of shame wherever I go
Always a voice vibrates behind the curtain
And I work with a dead heart
I turn away as the machine tramples a gentle lady

The landscapes of a hurricane mind are sacred to their
owners
I saw the golden bars rising from behind the mountain
The rays sunk into my skin like fishhooks
Pulling me towards the light that I had forgotten
I could no longer hold any light

I carry with me a small piece of fool's gold
Far away from the treasure chest in the sky
My load drives me beneath the ground
Where I can savor its trappings for only a short period …
Until I have less than anything I could want

Beyond a box of anonymous body parts
I see flower children sweeping the hills
Their buck-toothed smiles delirious with hope

My biggest fear is to die with the keys in my hand
Bread makes butter ... it's the science of belief
Maybe a rubber band will turn up somehow
My lamb calls me home

Completed July 3, 2004

Die Blumen des Kapitalismus

***

Älterer Bruder – Sei mein Manager
Ein dermaßen Verlorener wie ich sollte nicht singen
Wo ist meine Babysitterin mit ihrem Rollstuhl?
Wo ist meine Lederjacke, mein Personalausweis?

Bin ich in Amerika ohne Computer obdachlos?
Ein Mann mit Pudel – kein reisender Roadie mit Ahnung
Ohne Saxophon
Ohne die Passanten ordentlich anzumachen ...

$$$

Erwartetest du größer zu werden, Desert Storm?

Während meine Nachbarn in Brooklyn von deiner
Skyline erfrischt werden

Ob Marke für Münze
Oder Münze des Feuers

Ob Münze des Benzins
Oder Feuer aus Benzin

Was sollte ich erwarten, Flut oder Omelett?

Versammelt euch, Gitarren-Mann, Sound-Mann
Dieb und Türsteher

Gitarren-Techniker und Penner-Punk (mit Petrolium-Iro)
Tauscht Marken auf den feinen Straßen Manhattans aus

Was sollte ich erwarten, eine Million Dollars oder einen
Gummiknüppel in meinen Arsch?
(Daß sich meine Haut zu Leder wandelt?)

Und meine Kehle mit Herzmuscheln gefüllt
Sind es deine Ohren, die dieses schreckliche Geräusch
erzeugen?
Ein nüchterner Folksinger wird sein Management retten

»Subjektivität brachte die unabhängige Plattenfirma um«

Con Edison ist der tyrannischste Lude unter uns

Kellnerin in Lumpen ... serviert dem betrunkenen
Folksinger Kuchen
Lesbischer Leichnam in einem Meer aus Schlagzeug-
schleifen begraben
Folksinger von Con Edison geschändet
Sein bluesiges Blut rinnt unerkannt durch die Gossen
seiner Website
Sauberer als die Platintränen eines Wunderbabys

Lude Jerusalems – laß uns sie zusammenschlagen mit
unseren Tomahawks in stürmisch aufgewalltem
Haschischrauch

Im Land der Dyckman Straße
Wo die Eiskremgötter Seminare halten
für die Philosophen des Bezirks Westchester

Wo die hebräische Inschrift von der Matze schmilzt
ehrwürdig wie ein Süßholzfleck auf den Khakis eines
Heckenschützen

Wo die kandierte Vegetation vom Inneren erschlagen wird

Faulpelz Zyperns

Und die Gliedmaßen des Folksingers baumeln von Angelruten entlang des Ufers des Hudson
(72 Leagues unter dem Taubenauge)

Mal dir den vampiristischen Ochsenfrosch aus, der den prähistorischen Tumor der 9th Street auslutscht

Glotz das Königshaus von Las Vegas an – dessen Ökonomie übergeschnappt ist ...

Der Flugzeugtreibstoff versengt unsere Ochsenfroschzungen
so bitter wie Crystal Meth ohne Gewissensprüfung

1. »Wie können wir ficken?« lächelt sie,
am Kantstein unseres genitalen Knotenpunkts kauernd

2. »Ich habe eine Immunität gegen den Zauber der Nacht entwickelt«, lächelt sie,
über den Gleichmut ihrer versauten Festplatte nachdenkend

... immun gegen Huckepackritte durch den Verkehr

Laßt Joe Camel die Außenpolitik aushandeln –
die werden einem Kamel vertrauen

Meine Liebe ist ein glitschiges rotes Ungeheuer, das
einschläft, bevor …

Ein Tourbus wird über die London Bridge geschickt
Im Innern des Fahrzeugs beobachten wir das neueste
Budweiser Simplex

Hinter der Bühne des Metropolitan Café ducken sich
die Abziehbilder unter ein blasses Modell von
Johnny Depp

Stämme und Flanken spicken das Depot, wo die
Aasfresser auf den himmlischen Joint stoßen

Die Aasfresser sind glitschige Draufgänger – zu gleichen
Teilen Pflanze und Tier

Zur Mahlzeit lassen wir einen Bronx-Schlachtruf an die
Ekligen Yankees raus

Ich lobe den Junkie-Babysitter
wenn ich von einer langen Reise nach Hause komme
um meine Lämmer im Bett vorzufinden – fest ein-
geschlafen
und nichts von dem Porzellan fehlt

Eine knusprige Zigarette brennt in des Piraten zitternder
Hand

Die Sturmwolken hängen unter dem Ungetüm von
einem Bohnenstengel
Er glaubt, er hört ein Geräusch aus seiner Garderobe
Er macht eine Geste in Richtung eines seiner zur See
fahrenden Mitarbeiter ...
... mit verheerenden Folgen

Desert Storm, ich rufe dich heute nacht aus den Archiven
der MTV News auf
Auf daß du am Abend im Yankee Stadion wiedererschei-
nen magst
In Armani gekleidet, Schecks über Tantiemen in deinen
Taschen
Orientalische Gutsel im Waschraum schnüffelnd
Gegen den journalistischen Gedächtnisschwund prote-
stierend, der die westliche Welt blendet

Desert Storm, ich nehm dich mit auf meine Tournee
Meine Religion wird dein Soundcheck sein
Ich werde durch deine knusprige Zigarette sprechen
Diese knusprige Zigarette, einbalsamiert mit dem Blut
des Stinktiers!

F: Wo ist Hussein heute morgen?
A: Studiert die Magna Carta mit abgebrühter Distanz

Jerusalem, ich sehne mich danach, wieder durch die
Wüsteneien deiner Einkaufszentren zu ziehen
Schwemme an an der Küste, Tripp Straße 79
Und verlange mein Königreich der verhedderten
Nintendo-Kabel zurück

Ich verweilte in den Parks
und unter den Brücken des erloschenen Jerusalem
magische Notizen verfassend …

… richtige Straßen hinunterfahrend
Händchen mit welchen aus meiner Klasse haltend
Enten fütternd
(ich habe Enten mein ganzes Leben lang reingelegt)

Ich habe die Übertragung meiner ins Gästebuch des
Columbia Hotel gekritzelten Hausaufgaben abge-
schlossen

Ich habe die Wiesen des Hyde Park auf der Suche nach
dem Schlüssel für die Mini-Bar durchkämmt …
den Strokes auf den Fersen

Ich habe die Wüsten verschwinden sehen
und die Obstplatten größer werden

Ich merke, wie sie die Begabung von Kimya Dawson,
Turner Cody und Diane Cluck übersehen

(Ring Nasan, Rick Shapiro)

Besonderer Dank an Juliet Joslin
von den Bewohnern Mount Kiscos, New York

Fertiggestellt am 5. August 2003

Der Zivilist

Refrain

1. Das Röhren der Massen in den Käfigen zur Linken
2. Stränge von Autos binden sich vorbei
3. Nimm deine Hand und wische die Tränen von meinen weinenden Bibelaugen
4. Wir hatten einen Drachen, zu schmeißen nach ihm Sachen
5. Treib diese Johnnys
6. Diese Entscheidung zieht Licht aus dem Fluß
7. Ich starb unvollendet und bewußtlos
8. Eine gesunde Portion Sand blieb in meiner Atmung stecken
9. Dame, ihr Blut auf den Strand hustend
10. Ich stellte auch fest, daß jeder gültige Bonus seine »für immer«-Qualität besitzt
11. Ich werde keine Midlife-crisis haben
    (weil ich eine Midchildhood-crisis hatte)
12. Genieß es, mißbrauch es nicht, Hippies fürchten sich nicht vor dem Tod!
13. Ricki macht dem König so viele Komplimente, daß der König Ricki verspeist
14. Der Sommer kommt rein und weint
15. Bullenfisch saß auf einem Felsen und feuerte seine Sekretärin
    (»Ich könnte mich dran gewöhnen«, sagte er)
16. New York City ist mein Fusselsieb
17. New York kommt rein wie Wind
    (und bläst meinen Hut wieder runter)

18. *Oh, die Freude, angesehen zu werden*
Oh, die Freude, zurückzusehen
Oh, die Freude, Verkehr zu regeln
Pack mir eine Tüte für 20 Dollars
19. Schnall den Flipper an den Hammel
20. Ich dachte an gelbe Rechtecke, als eine Bombe explodierte und meinen Schwanz um den Berg herumschleuderte
21. Captain Noodle lebte unter einer Brücke
22. Jemand stürzte den Tütenmann
23. Schneid mir ein Stück von deinem sauren Kuchen ab
24. Eine Hexenjagd in der Stadt trennt Captain Noodle von Dixie
25. Ein Historiker liest ein politisches Magazin falsch und plädiert weise für eine andere Wirklichkeit
26. Eine Bombe löst Blitz aus, die Intelligenz zu erhöhen
27. Springsteens »Schmollippen«-Foto löst Tamtam in der Boulevardpresse aus und bringt ihm einen Plattenvertrag ein
28. James Brown reist nach Indien
(Geburtenrate steigt um 0,09% pro Familie)
29. Boston Crème Tampon
30. Mord erhöht den Wert von Jeffreys Aktien
31. Jeffrey stellt Dixie ein, um ein Fresko auf das Dach seines Gewölbes zu malen
32. Universal Sucka (Gummigeschosse)
33. Die Symptome schmecken nach Cola
(Liebesinfektion)
34. Sie kommt spät raus, wenn die Nacht am dunkelsten ist
35. Teilzeithippie / Vollzeitnutte

36. Liebe zwischen Cousins, Cousinen
(leicht, darauf herumzuhacken)
37. Eine Flasche U-Bahn-Saft
38. Deine Schultern sind einfach Griffe, wenn ich dich
von hinten ficke
39. Geboren, um prima zu sein
40. Er könnte mich aus meinem Knochenheim pflücken
41. Nächstern Morg'n
42. Im Bett mit Roger
(im Bett mit einem alten, kranken Freund)
43. Vor eines Zauberers Möse zurückschrecken
(mit den Paparazzi ganz rumgewickelt)
44. Setz deinen Kopffelsen auf (Leg deine Arschuhr an)
45. Eine Schachtel Sahne
46. Neon AIDS (the kool AIDS)
47. Bootsmusik
48. Lagebedingter Blues
49. Ich sollte ein Polizeiboot beschaffen und es dem
Ozean mit der Hand besorgen
50. Gestern war Ostern und der Spielautomat hat gerade
geklingelt
51. Und unten landet ein Scheiß im Gesicht der
lächelnden Judy
52. Rauch meine Träume, bevor die Hämmer sie
ineinanderkneten
53. Die Unmöglichkeit, gute Stiefel zu finden,
konfroniert zwei Teenager ganz direkt
54. Kurbel es endlos an, für immer, ohne Grund
55. Mee-Haw!!! Mee-Haw!!!

Erste Strophe: Kibbuz

1. Arnid, der in einem Zelt vor dem Haus seiner Mutter lebt, bekommt irgendwie heraus, daß er Mitglied eines verlorenen Stammes Israels ist
2. Arnid befindet sich auf einer Mission Gottes (das Gegenteil von Gleichgewicht)
3. Menschen werden immer als mit den Tieren benachbart beschrieben werden
4. Kann's gar nicht erwarten, einundzwanzig zu werden
5. Zu viele gebrochene Herzen in meinem Kopf

Zweite Strophe: Wir sorgten dafür, daß dein Geist uns beleidigt

1. Wir schufen deinen Geist, damit er uns beleidigt
2. Mein Format hat sich zum Schlechten entwickelt
3. Ich will mein Stück Kuchen wegschmeißen
4. Das Telefon steht bei der Tür (ein Auto, das teure Kleider trägt)
5. Löcher zwischen den Seiten

Dritte Strophe: Wenn die Staubkugeln sich am Morgen setzen

1. Der Wachsrückzieher (eine Kanone namens Sohn)
2. Wir tanzen durch ein Labyrinth aus Millionen peinlicher Tage
3. Kleiner toter Vogel, der scheußlich und reglos daliegt
4. Die Krankheit, zu der du wurdest (wo alles so unaufrichtig wirkt)

5. Vögel einatmen und Knochen ausspucken
6. Dein Gesicht küssen (mein Lieblingsprojekt)
7. Zeig mir ein Waisenkind, und ich zeige dir einen
Computer, der weint

Vierte Strophe:
Du hast Löcher in deiner Hose,
aber die sehen gut aus

1. Hey, Tierhände!!
2. Besitze ich, was man braucht, um ungeschützt zu
sein?
3. Wie hätten wir realisieren können, daß wir gestorben
waren? (Herr, niemand nahm uns zur Seite)
4. Es ist brandneu alles!!
5. In einer Welt, wo nichts wirklich wahr ist
(was soll ein vertrauensseliger Kerl wie ich da tun?)
6. Papa war in Uniform da
7. Oh Baby, ich möchte dir etwas Schönes andrehen

Fünfte Strophe: Wir waren hart

1. Wir hatten einen Drachen, zu schmeißen nach ihm
Sachen
2. Ein Eichhörnchen rannte vorbei, ich weiß, was es
denkt (Ich bin okay wie die Welt)
3. Du willst deine Lehrer ficken
4. Mario kann fliegen!!
(Ich setze meinen Glücksrucksack auf)
5. Wir brauchen nicht mehr nach oben zu gucken,
um Gott zu danken

6. Ich ließ meine Drogenschachtel am Fuß der Striptease-Stange liegen

Sechste Strophe:
Alles passiert intuitiv

1. Die Zukunft riecht wie brennende Zähne
2. Mein Vogel gegen dein Nest
3. Verloren im Garten der fürstlichen Vergnügungen
4. Wir nehmen's (Der wahre Jakob)
5. Unterwirf deinen Körper der Gegenwart (Rück dein Bett raus)
6. Sogar Traubensaft hat Bedürfnisse
7. Ich möchte nie wieder einen Körper haben (sie werden dir nie erlauben, damit aufzuhören, den Fels zu rollen)
8. Mikrochips in ihren Fäkalien
9. Alle in Dreiergruppen (denken, Gott ist nur für sie zu sehen)
10. Ein Haufen Schauspieler auf einer Schrei-Konferenz
11. Die Tide steigt in deinem Schlafzimmer
12. Folge dir in deinen Schlafzimmerladen
13. Ich dachte, alles wäre umsonst (bis ich mich im Gefängnis wiederfand)
14. Wert ist schön
15. Die Vergewaltigungen waren so bösartig (aber die Knabbermischung war köstlich)
16. Adam Green
17. Ich werde meine Schuhe weggeben, ich hoffe, ich möchte sie nicht zurückhaben

Siebte Strophe:
Ich fühle mich nur wohl,
wenn ich wie ein Arschloch angezogen bin

1. Sich wie eine Drag Queen fühlen
(sich wie ein Zwischending fühlen)
2. In Teppiche schlechten Atems gekuschelt
(Gags auspinkelnd)
3. Irrtümer der Zunge
(deren Lispeln mich kommen läßt)
4. Aus dem Schritt kriechen (Kirschen in Unterhosen)
5. Du bist, was du nicht hören möchtest
6. Selbst, wenn ich überall sein könnte
(würde ich immer noch da sein müssen)
7. Ich wurde geboren, ich weinte
(ich lebte ein Leben, ich starb)
8. Adam Green weiß andere zu schätzen
(ich seh so spitze gespiegelt in deinen Augen aus)
9. Wer zählt?

Achte Strophe:
Pokemon kaubares Ritalin

1. Pokemon kaubares Ritalin
2. Der Stuhl war so riesig wie ein Gebäude
3. In der geheimen Werkstatt des Präparators
(gibt es einen mit dreckigen Socken ausgestopften Milliardär)
4. Ich erzählte die Geschichte meines Lebens, stolperte und stürzte auf ein Messer
5. Ich schau den Tunnel hinab zu ihr, und sie winkt zurück

6. Schieß dein Gesicht zu Tode
(irgendein toter Kerl mit »echtem Gesicht«)
7. Vielen Dank, daß du diesen Pilz meinem Fuß ausgehändigt hast
8. Wie weit kann ich meine Liebe beugen
(und wissen, sie wird mich zurückküssen?)
9. Ich möchte andere Organismen zerreißen
(haariges Plastik)
10. Ich muß dieses Stück Scheiße hinter die Affenstatue legen
11. Lederhimmel, aus Himmel gemacht
(Lederregen, aus Regen gemacht)
12. Spiel ein paar Zeitspiele
(spiel vielleicht ein bißchen Zeitbombe)
13. Information ist eine müffelnde braune Kreation
14. Rote Backsteine fallen aus deiner Vagina
15. *Carolina (sie ist aus Texas)*
Ihre Lippen schmecken wie gesunkene Schiffe
(ihre Brüste schmecken wie Frühstück)
16. Sie könnte mich durch den Münzfernsprecher lutschen
17. Du kannst den Boden nicht hereinlegen

Neunte Strophe:
Ich kann nicht arbeiten

1. Reden ist billig
(aber mehr habe ich nicht zu verkaufen)
2. Ich kampierte draußen im Fahrstuhl
3. Du kannst dich voll durch sie neigen
(Du kannst dich zu ihnen ficken)

4. Sag mir, hast du sein Lied angehört?
(War es so gut, daß du dabei masturbieren mußtest?)
5. Ich will'n Pferd mit Krücken reiten
6. Sie setzen dich in die Ecke zurück, wo sie dich füttern
7. Ich bringe die ganzen Speisekarten in die Sauställe
(ich lache um das Holz, wenn die Axt stirbt)
8. Gesiebt mit Schuld (gebratpfannt mit Milch)
9. Vorsichtig öffne ich die Tür jedem neuen Kuß,
der durchkommt
10. Laß uns anfangen, indem wir erst mal beenden
11. Er hat 1000 Tage lang nichts mehr gesagt

Zehnte Strophe:
Ich warf einen flüchtigen Blick
auf das neue Du

1. Wir verließen das Badehaus
(bau dein Haus nicht in den Korridor)
2. Jede Bestrafung ist ein Stück Tod
(Ich war stets ihr Lieblingspatient)
3. Du bist ein freier Wanderer
(Du erreichst, daß sie an deiner Zunge lutschen)
4. Ich sah das tote Kind im Teich (und das sind wir)
5. Ich nahm eines ihrer lockigen roten Haare
(und fügte es meinen eigenen hinzu)
6. Maschinerie der Nacht
7. Drück Play und mach diese Party an
8. Geschäft blüht (aber Geldsack lebt allein)
9. Zigaretten für die Guten rauchen

Überleitung

1. New York City trug sein Brautkleid
2. Der Garten melkt ein Kind
(unter der grünen Glühbirne)
3. Berge aus Wein schwimmen unter den wäßrigen
Laken
4. Drahtrahmen aus schartigen Brustwarzen, an Saiten
aus Wind aufgehängt
5. Lieder der geringfügigen Erfahrung
(ein Computer war mein Christoph K.)
6. Times Square war meine Schierlingstanne
7. All meine Seiten sind zugleich aufgeschlagen
(helle Lichter auf alter Haut)
8. Ich ging ins Krankenhaus (um gut nachzudenken)
9. Blind wie ich sterblich war (fiel ich zum Licht)
10. Wenn ich einen kleinen Jungen ficken würde,
unwissentlich (versehentlich), würde ich es so tun:
a) konstant masturbieren
b) meine Träume vergessen
11. Spiegel im Heuhaufen
12. Ich masturbierte so häufig, daß mich meine rechte
Hand verließ. (Also begann ich, meine linke Hand zu
benutzen. Und meine linke Hand *rechte mich*!)
13. Ich lehne mich zurück wie ein Sultan (und betrachte
die Vorführung deines blauen Schattens)
14. Ich erwarte nicht, daß ich jemals wieder abspritze
15. Ich kannte einen Bauer, der seine Kinder schlug
(um seinen Mais mit ihren Tränen zu wässern)

Elfte Strophe:
Brot im Bett

1. Dinge, die ich morgen brauche: Job, Seife, Handtuch, Decke, Becher, Lichtschalter, Vordertür
2. Hilf mir, Papa, Mama mag es nicht, wenn ich in ihrer Unterwäsche herumspiele
3. New York ist verheiratet, aber sie will immer noch einen letzten Kuß
4. Ich vergaß in dieser Minute 59 mal, daß ich dich liebe
5. Lauf die 1st Street runter und spiel einen G-Akkord (Dann lauf die 2nd Street runter und spiel einen C-Akkord)
6. Die Cowboys wurden dort von den Indianern verführt
7. Pandoras Zigaretten stehlen
8. *Wir trafen John auf der Bootsausstellung*
   (mit auf ihn gerichteten Pfeilen)
   Er nannte uns eine Nummer
   (nach Woodstock folgten wir)
9. Wir brauchen gesunde Soldaten, um sie auf fleischiger Leinwand zu verfolgen
   (die Büchse menschlichen Salats)
10. Des Himmels Salat anmachen

Zwölfte Strophe:
Ich liebe dich selbst

1. Treib diese Trudys und Judys und Moes
   (treib diese Johnnys den ganzen Weg heim)
2. Sie trieb diese Johnnys durch einen Korridor unterhalb ihres Zuhauses

3. Wer ließ eine Roofoo in mein Gingeroo gleiten?
4. Treib diese Regenbögen
5. Knochen im Pudding (Kinder in der Fischsuppe)
6. Mehr wie ein Künstler ist weniger wie eine Dame
7. Dixie kam nach New York, um eine berühmte Raverin zu werden
8. Die Triumphe der Maden (Spritzer von Tarantulas)
9. Der Boden ist alles, was die Reichen nicht berühren müssen
10. Sturz der Liebe

Dreizehnte Strophe: Sie ist ne alte Krähe

1. Ein grüner Nylonhummer
2. Ich sprühe meine Geometrie
3. Knarrenkumpel
4. Ich habe ein Hinken in meinem kosmischen Schlurfen
5. Nokay

Vierzehnte Strophe: Sonnentage im Schlachterbüro

1. Himbeerholzmösen (Sandpapierkokomo)
2. Grüne Filzvagina
3. Meine großen, knolligen Finger, sie machen all meine kleinen Freunde kaputt

Fünfzehnte Strophe:
Ich traf Chad auf dem Phish-Konzert

1. Blind in den tiefsten Rachen langen
   (im braunsten Teil der Stadt)
2. Die Bettlerhand: ein Loch ohne Boden
   (schnall einen Beiwagen an meinen linken Fuß)

Bonusstrophe:
Das Bronzedenkmal kitzeln

1. Mein Leben als jemand, der Kathy gefickt hat, die AIDS hatte
2. Tagtäglich entkomme ich durch das goldene Gitter

Sechzehnte Strophe:
Klebe ein Pferdebein an mein Gemälde

1. Ich habe vorhin gerade einen Schnapsladen ausgeraubt
2. Tiere sprießen wie Speichen aus seiner Krone
3. Verschütte die Bohnen, bis sie brechen
4. Masturbation – mein eigener Bürgerkrieg
   (während du auf Zehenspitzen meinen Indianer umrundest)
5. Die Asche zwischen meinen Zehen
6. Ich traf den König (und er signierte meine Flügel)
7. Wir zischen durch das Wirrwarr der Nacht
   (nur, um das falsche Licht des Morgens zu begrüßen)
8. (Körbchen, Körbchen)
9. Im Bett mit einer Rosine
   (im Bett mit einem alten, kranken Freund)

10. Meine Schlagzeugmaschinenkanonenflöte
11. Die fleckig behaarte Schönheit
12. Laß einfach meine müden Finger über die goldenen Bühnen ihres Körpers wandern
13. Ich erschoß meine Straße (wenn jetzt ist jetzt ist jetzt ist jetzt ist jetzt)
14. Rosa Landstraßen (Tee und Verkehr)
15. Bau einen Mund ohne Makel (überquere eine Straße im Zorn)
16. Bau deine eigene Vagina (denke an ein neues Bierdosendesign)
17. Reit die Karotten den Hügel runter (dem Neonhummer davonrennen)
18. Britney Spears stieg vom Himmel herab und zeichnete eine Linie in den Sand
19. Meine Knochen, wie sie gegen den raffiniert verschlüsselten Flaum klappern
20. Augen, die Armeen zum Glühen bringen
21. Ich presse mich auf ihr Schwert nieder
22. Steckte meinen Schwanz in einen Revolver (Gott sei Dank machte es klick)

Siebzehnte Strophe: Vor dem Spiegel hängengeblieben

1. Meine verurteilte Zukunft macht Anstalten, stellt, als sie konvergiert, fest, daß sie obdachlos ist
2. Fab war sauer auf seine Freunde, daß sie nicht zuließen, daß er sie beschützte (also tat er sich selber weh)
3. Wenn der Tod als Zimmermann eintritt (möchte ich Sex mit der Zeit haben)

4. Die Innereien eines Käfers schmecken nach Erdbeeren.
(Die Innereien eines Pferds schmecken nach Erdnußbutter)
5. *Wie eine kaputte Uhr, die über eine leere Drogenschachtel lacht*
Wie ein Entenficker, der sich für einen Sack Entenschwänze entfacht
6. Du wirst niemals so schwarz sein wie ich
7. Der König ist auf Droge (gute Nacht, Licht)
8. Auf den Grund seines Liedes sinken
9. Der König küßt Spinnen
10. Sie reißt die Treppe von ihrer Vagina ab
11. Ich entführte dieses lässige Kind
12. Handele mir kaputte Uhren gegen gestohlene Bilder von Superman ein
13. Ich binde meinen Schwanz von deinem los
14. Britney Spears stieg vom Himmel herab und erstickte mit ihren muskulösen Schenkeln eine Kobra
15. Penisfieber
16. Freude über die Gratisfilmvorführung während des Flugs (Freude, Geld in einem Swimmingpool zu verdienen)
17. Ein Schwanz hat sich auf meinem obdachlosen Arsch ausgebreitet
18. Denk an all den Sex, den ich hätte haben können, während sie mich betrog
19. Ich möchte die Wahrheit über Sex mit Männern kennen
20. Diese Kinder schmecken wie Ungeheuer

Achtzehnte Strophe:
Auf meinem Weg ins sexuelle Verhängnis

1. Wie viele geschlechtliche Outlaws in diesem Raum?
2. Gerissene rote Spaßmacher, welche vom geilen Himmel regnen
3. Stecken ihre Schwänze in die mit Dornen gefüllten Beutel
4. Sie hatte einen heißen rassistischen Körper
5. Die Verbesserungen, die an den Passagieren durchgeführt wurden
6. Amerikanisches Schloß – die Lippen der Haustür (die Kaminfürze)
7. Honig an den Drähten
8. Annie nimmt sich die Haut der See und zieht sie wie ein Handtuch hinter sich her
9. Schmetterlingszinken
(reiten auf dem Trägenbogen ins Land der Träume)
10. Ich muß für die Yankees spielen (aber ich kann den Weg zum Spielfeld nicht finden)
11. Ich schwöre bei der Regierung, daß ich dich liebe
12. Schlauchende Quallen
13. Von der Firma empfohlenes Schicksal
14. Meine Mutter führte meinen Vater in mich ein
15. Rudere, rudere den U-Bahn-Waggon
(durch die russischen Felder)
16. Am Ende ließ Schwierigkeit ihren Busch aufblitzen und mich verkleidet zurück
17. Das Biest in mir
(hat einen Platz in der Gesellschaft gefunden)
18. Sie hat meine Muschi
(tief im Herzen des Einkaufszentrums)

19. Ihr Mund war zu groß, um mir einen zu blasen
(also wischte sie mir statt dessen den Arsch ab)
20. Den Sexualakt tarnen
21. Was mache ich in New York City?

Fertiggestellt am 11. September 2001

Strophe 12, Zeile 7 konzipiert von Jest Commons
Strophe 17, Zeile 2 geschrieben von Kimya Dawson
Strophe 17, Zeile 6 geschrieben von Emil Africa
Captain Noodle ist eine Figur, die von Jest Commons kreiert wurde

Gefrorene schwule Schildkröte

Die Lieder, die ich mir angewöhnte, um mich an Jesus zu gewöhnen
Abscheu vor der herrschenden Ersten Weltordnung –
Eine Perle wird aus einem blauen Unterstand hervorgeholt – zu dem ansehnlichen Kaiser gebracht und tief im Innern des Landes einsortiert
Meine Schwester – die Legende
Die Legende der Ordnung
Erinnerung der Dauerläufer auf der Tripp Straße
Deutsche beseitigen die Dauerläufer auf der Tripp Straße
Das Tier ist im JCPenney angekommen
Altertümliche Sexualität
Die verkrumpelten Eingänge kollidieren in der erbärmlichsten Mission
Die knipsenden Insektenhände
(wo die Tennisbälle auf feurigen Sockeln leben)
Verbrenn die Deutschen, aber denk daran, uns zu unterrichten, warum
Eine Weile vor der Zeit, als – sie sich eine dieser Pflanzenkrankheiten einfing
Naziwalfänger
Ein Beispiel aus der Computersprache:
Segne diesen jüdischen Computer
Jesus war ein Rockefeller
An Nixon – der am Ende Fanzeug an die ganzen Promihasser verkaufte
Die von mir verkauften Ninja Dicks besaßen Geschick, Muddafigga

Muddafigga haß dein Mudda
Schick diesen Dick aufs College
An Nixon – der am Ende ein Lied für jeden Dick am College schrieb
Der erschreckende Sprung von einem menschlichen Wesen zum anderen
Ganz so, wie der Ninja mein bester Kumpel wurde, während mein Körper aufs College ging
Ich habe meine Familie auf eine Art geregelt, welche die meisten Leute nie angemessen finden konnten
Mutter kann nicht in meine Wildnis blicken
Wo deren Brüste wie angemalte Schiffe in einem Oberschenkel-Hafen schwimmen
Vielleicht ein bißchen Geschmack des Hafens
Vielleicht noch ein Saft im Turm
Vielleicht noch ein Junge zum Abendbrot
Mich würde interessieren, ob sein Bart größer ist als sein Verstand
Ein Schmuckanhänger Gottes ist es, was da aus jedermanns Gehirn baumelt
Eine Frau ist ein Krankenhaus
Eifersüchtig auf jede Frau, die ich sehe
William hatte in keiner Szene eine Chance
Joey – komm her, Alter – mit deinem Postkoitus-Album, damit es alle sehen
Ich glaube, ich hörte die Mädchen auf der Frühstückfreßolympiade schlecht über ihn reden
Alle Künstler arbeiten an Karikaturen
Die Technik der weichen Zunge
Oh, wie das Wasser im Mund vor Verlangen nach mehr Mund zusammenläuft

Alle Liederschreiber sind zu einem gewissen Grad
schwul
Liste der Komplexe:
Ich möchte mit allen Leuten, die ich kenne, sexuelle
Erfahrungen haben
(sei es auch nur, daß sie die Haare des Wunderkinds
kämmen, das mich berührt)
Stellt man seiner zweiten Mutter wegen Sex nach?
Dies ist eine der widerstandsfähigsten Gehirnhäute, die
ich je ganz durchgeschnitten gesehen habe
Also erzähl uns nicht, daß du deine ganze Pisse zwischen
den Decken verborgen hast
Jameson-Schnaps enthüllt – der Porno-Star lebt mit drei
Fans zusammen
Zeit für ein Quiz – Wessen Sex rechtfertigt unser eigenes
Leben?
Deutsche Sex-Story: Die Blonde biß in den Kubaner
Other Music – ein Laden mit enormem Weitblick
Und Kim's ist auch ein bemerkenswert visionärer Laden
Die geschwollenen Tasten eines gebeutelten Laptop
Keuschball – das Spiel, das ein zölibatärer Mann spielt
Probleme, auf die wir beide stoßen: die Geschichte im
Lot halten
Schnell die Vergangenheit wieder zusammensetzen und
an die jaulenden Münder verfüttern
Einer von uns lehnte sich an den hölzernen Zaun eines
Gehöfts – »Was für eine großartige Kacke, Mann,
klassischer Scheiß!«
(während der Mann zum Hallo gelangt)
Ich möchte nicht sterben, verstanden?
Stellt mir irgendwelche Forderungen

Gebt mir paar Storkies, ich brauch mehr Storkies
Für ihn bin ich mein Bruder
Die krumpelnden Papiertürme
Hier ist meine Telefonnummer, komm rüber und geil
mich auf
Die krumpelnden Papierhosen eines
Kinderpornographen
Jedes Opfer in der Stadt braucht ein Exemplar
Eine Nase wackelt im Arsch
Mein Bett fällt aus meinem Bett
Die Schrift auf den Zehen
Die Zeiten, wenn ihre Gnade sich zeigt
Wieder für immer
An meine Eltern – ich erbte jedes Stück eurer Feigheit
Modestecker
Gespenster in den Sofakissen
Ich würde niemals echt jemanden umbringen –
ich würde nichts mit der Sauerei zu tun haben wollen
Kann eine Regierung Verliebte sein?
Herr Schwarzbrenner verbringt den Winter im
Gefängnis
Das Gebrüll der Massen ist ihm im Gefängnis Gesang
Das neue Manhattan
Das Buch der toten Gammler
Levi's Punk Rock Jeans mit aktuellen
Neon-Reißverschluß-Rockertaschen
Die neue Fernsehserie boy@house stellt einen der
grundlegenden Kurse in der Gefühlserziehung deines
Kindes dar
Idee zu einem Stück:
Ein Junge tut sich schwer an der Michael Jordan

Universität. Zu seinem Geburtstag kauft ihm sein
Vater »Das Buch der toten Gammler«
Er ist tot in der Hinsicht, daß ihn niemand braucht
Wir müssen uns deine Jeans für die
Punk Rock-Ausstellung ausleihen
Einige Sicherheitskräfte suchen nach einem Mann.
»Hört auf, mich zu suchen!« ruft er
Ich werde die Titten von dem klebrigen Eis
runterlutschen
Der Kacka-Klatscher-Laden
Unter Menschen ist es beliebter, Hummer zu essen als
Meerschweinchen
In zwanzig Jahren wird in Komödien Insektenfleisch
weiter verbreitet sein als SPAM und Hühnchen
zusammen!
Weil es da draußen mehr zu essen gibt als in Mägen
Things don't suck anymore ... they fuck!
Dieses Brötchen fickt
Kann die vom Ficken durchnäßte Regierung ein Stück
Metall durch eine glitzernde Harnröhre saugen?
Arthur starrte die Negerin an, als sie auf den
Flugzeugsitz schiß
Dieses Flugzeugessen fickt
Dieses Flugzeug fickt!

(*)

Ein Flugzeug zwischen den baumwollenen Laken – – –

(*)

Regierung ist ein Schwanzwort
Die wichtigste Geschichte, die jemals vergessen wurde

Ich steckte meinen Schwanz in ihren Keks, da fiel ihre
Füllung raus
Adam-und-Kimya-Fickbildchen
Für mein Leben würde ich gern was haben?
»Wer ist da auf dem Bildschirm, Schlampe?!?!«
Ich kann Freundschaften schließen
Regierung fickt
Hitlers Untergang lag darin, daß er den Reden, die er
hielt, glaubte
Ich kann mich nicht um die Heilung kümmern
Offenbar fürchte ich mich davor, verprügelt zu werden
Zerschlag einen Mythos
Einer der Gründe, weshalb ich möglicherweise
wegziehen werde
Ich trete in den Alligator
Werde dir einen brandneuen Abräumer kaufen
Werde dich die Treppen runter steuern
Wie heißt die Marke deines Boots?
Särge, auf denen »Oh, nein!« steht
Gegenstände fallen im Dunkeln runter
Steven Jesse Bernstein hatte einen bedeutenden Einfluß
auf mein Leben
»Es steckt eine gewisse Lyrik im Lustspiel«
(Es steckt ein gewisses Lustspiel in Kakteen)
Ich kann diese Bänder nur beobachten
Das sind nur Insider-Witze, weil die Außenwelt mit
ihnen nicht vertraut ist, stimmt's, Roger?
Insider-Witz-Videos
Wenn wir genug vom System verstehen, um es zu reiten
Du hoffst also, die Leute, die heiraten, sind aufeinander
angewiesen anstatt einfach nur tot

Glotz in deinen inneren Nigger
Ich muß meine E-mails checken, nachsehen, ob Bruce
Springsteen mir geantwortet hat
Das Wort »care« hat sechs verschiedene Bedeutungen
Gib mir einen Zoll Geld
Mit Geld besetzte Pferde
(mit Zigaretten besetzte Seeleute)
Das Echo des Fleisches meiner Mutter
Die Drogen der tödlichen Vergangenheit
Der Deckenpropeller beginnt zu blubbern
Ich bin so wie sie sich früher fühlte
»Ich log den Arzt an. Ich sagte ihm, ich rauchte kein
Hasch«
Dennis leugnet den Fehler (ich leugne das Datum)
Jeder klopfte mir auf den Rücken, als ich sie mit
geschlossenen Augen küßte
Von einer Stadt berührt
J-Los unendliche Weisheit
Immer gemeinsam in Richtung der Kamera blicken
Jeder, dessen Seele von der Kamera aufgesaugt wird,
sollte zurückschlagen und sich selbst eine Kamera an-
schaffen
Laß uns eine Kamera holen und diese Fucks töten!
Und so wird jedem einzelnen seine Welt rausgesaugt
Ich saug deine Welt aus dir raus
Zeit, daß wir uns eine eigene Kamera besorgen
Als das Zelt ausrutscht und die Fetzen zu unserer Bleibe
werden
Und das Boot segelt hinab in den morastigen Grund
So wie ein Kind eine emotionale Wirkung auf den Lehrer
ausübt, übt ein schlechter Verbraucher eine
emotionale Wirkung auf Winona Ryder aus

Gefangen in einer Geschlechtskrankheitsfestung
Ihre Hosen fielen runter und sie machten ihr Geschlecht
hinten wieder dran
Heutzutage steht eher das Individuum im Mittelpunkt
(Scheißdreck!)
Ein Bühneneichhörnchen
Teenage Mutant Ninja Eichhörnchen
And'r Eichhörnchen, für and're Schildkröten
Top 10 Übelste Augenblicke des Jahres:

1. In einem Schildkrötenkragenpullover auf einer
Pop-Art-Totenfeier gelyncht werden
2. Die schwule Schildkröte in einen Eisblock eingefroren auf dem Gipfel des Olymp finden

Dermaßen häufig besuche ich meine Piratenfreunde,
daß sie kaum je bemerken, daß ich weg bin
»Gefrorene schwule Schildkröte« ist ja so ein Hermes-Abklatsch!
Mein Ziel scheint zu sein, sie zu verwandeln und dann
auszurangieren
Augen, die nach mehr Armeen auf ihren breiten
Fernsehschirmen verlangen
Ich werde das »Unterwegs« für meine Generation
schreiben. Es wird »Bleib zu Hause« heißen
Las-Vegas-Nadelstreifen
Der Schuhfanatiker belästigt Slipper in Vegas
Im Hinblick auf deinen Anruf
Im Hinblick auf eine Zeit, in der ein falscher Mausklick
zu einem üblen Geruch führen wird
»Lincoln bezahlte Wilkes Booth, damit er ihn ermordete,
weil er sich für ihre schwule Liebesaffäre schämte und
nicht als der einzige schwule Präsident, den es je gab,
weiterleben wollte!«

Ich weiß die Hämatologie hier zu schätzen
Die Göttin der Twin-Soldaten
Ihre Finger sind phantastisch
Der Wind soll sarkastisch wehen
Ihre Zunge ist wie eine Bürste
Mein Schwanz ist wund von dem Versuch,
    diese Stegosaurusknochen zu ficken
Die Freiheit der Infizierten
Die Hosen brachen auf dem Teppich zusammen
Dadurch daß sie Ärzte waren, wurden sie zu Liebhabern
    ihrer Patienten
(Wir brauchen alle eine Kamera usw. ...)
Die Knechtschaft der Zufriedenheit
Mein Körper sollte drei Fürzen widerstehen können,
    ohne sich auf einsamen Pfaden zu zerstreuen
Mein Körper schimpft sich selber aus – wegen seines
    Wunschs nach Kontrolle
Mein Körper ist eine Komödie
    (ein Skelett eines Ninja-Priesters)
Meine Seele ist Fürze
Ninja-Jesus (Befall ihn in seinem Himmelhochlokal mit
    seinem Ninja Toast und Vögeln)
Mädchen sind einfach Jungen mit Vaginas
Auf einer Welle zurückgebliebenen asiatischen Sounds
    fliege ich zu den Mädchen zurück
Das tiefe dunkle Familiengeheimnis
Die Reflexe der Vernunft
(eine Träne fällt auf einen mit Trümmern gefüllten
    Rucksack)
Wie viele Zimmer in deiner Tasche?
Ein Bild aus Paste verbrennen

Sie wird einfach so lange über den Fluß fliegen,
bis eine Brücke sie durchschneidet
»Oh, wie ich diesen Zeh so sehr vermisse« von Dr. Seuss
Seit sie mir diese Videos gezeigt hat, bleibt nichts mehr
zu sagen
Insektenpenis-Tauschkarten
Die Gebräunten in einer weißen Welt
(mit dem gestohlenen Himmel vermählt)
Der Hunger fickt dich, während er dich ißt
Box ihre Vagina, bis sie ans College glaubt
Daß du nicht eifersüchtig sein solltest, heißt ja noch
nicht, daß sie nicht erstaunlich ist

Ein Telefoninterview mit dem Folksinger:

Sing Out!: Wo bist du gerade?

Folksinger: Ich bin in einem staubigen Raum. Ich bin voll auf Acid, Jim.

Sing Out!: Wie würdest du deine Musik beschreiben?

Folksinger: Die Leute verstehen nicht, wie mathematisch sie ist. Wie Mathematik auf meine Musik zutrifft. Wie in allen Wissenschaften, entsteht aus dem Ausschuß Gold. Ich glaube, es wären gute Lieder, um sie im Gefängnis zu singen.

Sing Out!: Also arbeitest du hart an den Liedern?

Folksinger: Wow, da hast du wirklich den Steifen aus seinem Sarg gezogen.

Sing Out!: Versteh ich nicht.

Folksinger: Ich bin wie ein Musik-Nazi. Nicht Menschen ... Musik. Ich bin ein kompromißloser Künstler.

Sing Out!: Was sind deine musikalischen Einflüsse?

Folksinger: Ich denke, die Leute sollten anfangen, die Mathematik ein bißchen mehr zu schätzen. Die Leute

realisieren nicht, daß Satan auch ein Engel ist.
Sing Out!: Was sind deine Pläne für die Zukunft?
Folksinger: Ich weiß es nicht. Ich muß gehen, Zeit für
meine Verabredung.
Es gibt ein Ungeheuer, das im Einkaufszentrum lebt
(und es haßt kleine Mädchen)
Bomben im Central Park (von der Sonne geschobene
Rollstühle)
Verstell bitte nichts an dieser Skala (denn dieses Radio
kennt Gefühle)
Alte Jungen lassen sich Bärte wachsen
»Einer meiner größten Einflüsse war Nickelodeon«
Noch nie eine nettere Falle erwischt (hört sich wie deine
Ohren an)
Probe deine Vormittage
Tiefgefrorene Mantras (Die Sandalen werden um die
Zehen der Statue herum dicker)
Lizenzen keimen   Keime entschuldigen sich
Kristallnachbildungen
Kaltes Gas und Messingblut   Unerklärlich gut entwickelt
Liebeskrank durch eine Regenfront rennen
Geister Afrikas
Fraktionen, sich bekämpfend   Fedrige Dreadlocks
Flüchtlinge, saubergeschrubbt   Primitives Seidensieb
Fötale Politik   Ein herzzerreißender Zurückgebliebener
Diplomatisches Gedränge   Verschmähte Eiserne Lunge
Küß mich, Nachmacherin
Vergewaltige mich heimlich   Geriatrischer Fluch
Miniserienväter
Gefrorenes Restaurant   Laserapfellachen
Himmlische Fischschwänze

Körperschlösser Im Ghetto dieses Hauses
Geschwollene Gummispießgesellen Gabardinefluch
Rocky Mountain-Marmelade Westliche Galaxien
Geranienpferdestärken Abgedroschenem Kauderwelsch
nachgeben Hedonistischer Moschus
25-Cent-Krankenhaus Schlafwandlerparadies
Freiluftparade
Im Paradies ausgesetzt Entführ die Parade
Der Meister der Drogen Giftnadelraucher
Pulsierendes Orakel Kosmonautenschwadron
Fötale Astronauten Gefrorenen Nektar rauchen
In einer Tüte Nervengas ertrinken Frischwasserkerker
Nuklearpriesterin Preisgekrönter Kerker
Ein Florida drei Blocks zurückfahren
Abpackbetriebskampf
Sauerstoffgutschein Rennpferd der Liebe
Amerikanischer Kuß
Mein Bruder – der Prophet Pfennighuhn
Autistische Nutte Sahniger englischer Mund
Suppiges Gerippe
Eine tiefere Seele suchen, um sie zur Zündung zu bringen
Länder aussortieren
Brummende Raketenträger Üppige Gerüchte
Kurbel den Karneval an
Lederallerheiligstes Elektrischer Bandit
Perfekte Attrappe
Mülldeponiebaby Seesternspaghetti Styroporsäulen
Siamesischer Krabbenjunge Neolithischer Fluch
Sicherheit inmitten einer Bezahlzone
Eine Ehe, die über die Zustimmung von Freunden
hinausgeht

»Mein Mantel hat mehr Löcher als Pittsburghs
Verteidigung«
Zwischen Preisen
Ein magersüchtiger Putto
Eine Hand aus dem Wald langte in das Taxi
Bagelherz (verlang die Flut zurück)
Ein Stück von dieser Tür ist noch immer in meinem
Herzen
Vom Freund zum Bewunderer (Person zu Tier)
Ein gebildeter Traum (der getoastete Augenblick)
Mein Bett ist eine Platte
Der Engel erwachte mit Seife in seinen Flügeln
Ich war weg, im Krieg (in der Buchhandlung)
Mit meinen Augen gegen das Bücherregal gedrückt
Und der silbergesichtige Chinese zeichnet sich hinten ab
Ein zerrissenes Gewand, über die Magna Carta drapiert
Hinter mir ist ein römisches Telefon angeschwollen
Tierhände, nach Riemen greifend (pelzige Finger,
zögernd)
Stämme aus Basketbällen (die Gebrauchsanweisung zum
Einkaufszentrum)
Ein Insektenherz donnert aus dem Zentrum eines jeden
Mikrophons
Die Riemen werden von elektrischen Rankenfußkrebsen
bewegt
Ich speiste heute abend mit dem silbergesichtigen
Schlägertyp – er verkonsumierte den Großteil des
Käferleichnams
Jeder Elternteil schickte sein Kind den Fluß runter, und
im Delta wurden sie sortiert
Brot in Ketten

Jeder Laden ist ein Verdächtiger
(jedes Schaufenster ist verstopft)
Langsam verliebte ich mich in meine Kanone
Eine Beerdigung aus der Sicht von unten
Als ich das letzte Mal geprüft wurde, konnte ich die Farben der UN-Flagge nicht erinnern
Seit ich mit einem kaputten Joystick herumlaufe, führe ich mein Leben im Notfallmodus
Notfallphantasie (unheilbare Vorhersage)
»So gut bin ich gar nicht, aber mir geht's extrem gut«
Spießige Katzen Übernatürliche Blumen Abs Pritzen
Seelischer Stuntman
»Nichts besser, als einem Riesenfreund den Buckel runterzurutschen«
Schach mit meiner Seele spielen (oder keine Seele hat mich)
Neurologie ist mir wichtiger als Lieder schreiben
(ich plansche in Sex)
Gefrorene schwule Schildkröte: die Geschichte von Bob Dylan
Anhang:
Ich bin am Ende meiner Latte
Betrachte ihn, wie er durch die Frauen geht, keinen Blick für irgendeinen Mann übrig hat
Zwei Männer umarmen sich im Eingang ihres Landhauses
Die vierte Haut der Nacht
(der Mond ist aufs College gegangen)
Oh, wie ich von Couch zu Couch zog
(oh, wie ich von Mond zu Mond stolperte)
Diese Mädchen kommen gern langsam runter
(überlegener Blues)

Die Vereinigten Säcke der Angst
Scheiß nicht auf meinen Sonnenschein
    (mit deinem verfickten Gesicht)
Ich sang, damit ich den Terror nicht fühlte
    (Helen Keller auf Acid)
»Ich weiß nicht genug über die Chinesen, um dich einen
    Rassisten nennen zu können«
Der Wind ist die Seele des Planeten
Vor dem Hotel wird der Transporter beladen
Hardcorekrankheitskanal
Löcher in den Flugzeugschwingen küssen
Mit einem Rock-Kritiker, der meine Hand hält,
    unternehme ich eine Tour durch mein Heimatland
»Ich bin allergisch auf Handschläge«
    (ich möchte die weiche Seele töten)
Nasses Handtuch in einem Gefrierfach
        Aluminiumschnurrbärte   Klopapierzigaretten
Eine Orgie des Lichts (ein Jahrhundert des Zweifels)
Ausländische Jungs haben die größten Schwänze
    (schweinische Witze)
Party in meinem Rucksack – Es ist ein Buch über ein
    Schwanzlutschen, das zum Lebensstil wurde
»Ich fing eine Nase im Voicestream«
Cowboysauce
Das tote Mädchen weint auf dem Boden des Brief-
    umschlags (ihr königlicher Mösenfurz)
Blut, das Löcher durch Blut boxt
Verblaßte Top-Ten-Liste in einer staubigen Ruhmeshalle
Ging genau vor meiner Show in ein Bordell
    (aber die Nutte holte mir zu langsam einen runter)
Die Freude, jemanden gemeinsam zu kennen

»Leute, die deine Scheiße küssen wollen, bevor du sie runterspülst«
Sommerblutergüsse (ich erschauere in einem Orgasmus der Angst)
Die Innenräume des Schmerzes
Ich kann hören, wie du dich im anderen Zimmer selbst verwertest
Eine besondere Sorte amerikanischen Eingeborenenhumors
Sternenkrank (der Papst machte in den Thron)
Verhandle mit der Krankheit

Fertiggestellt am 24. Dezember 2002

8 Seiten für Allah

*** Teil 1 ***

Google-Suche: Farmer Dave
Suchergebnisse (10-20, ansteigend)
10. Farmer Dave: Prominentenprofil – eine erstklassige Einrichtung der faulen Völker bei der Magisches Amerika GmbH
11. »Das ist einer der frühesten Träume, die ich erinnern kann«, führt Dave an, »ich bin mit meiner Geliebten bei McDonald's …«

Zwischen Duschficks holten wir Farmer Dave in seiner Genfer Gemeinde ein. > Google-Suche: Bagelherz

Tief im Herzen der jüdischen Wildnis …

Die Kriegstrommeln dröhnen, während Häuptling
Bagelherz zur Predigt anhebt
Die Trommeln der Gleichheit, schlagt sie mit aller Kraft
Tipis detonieren hinter dem Schamanen …
Wampum sprüht raus wie Popcorn

Einstmals, nach einer gescheiterten Ehe
Sprang ein Fan schreiend auf die Bühne
Wie ein Blitz grapschte sie das sterbende Kind
Und zog sich nach Israel zurück

Wir sind ECHTE INDIANER aus den Wäldern
Einheimischer als unsere Vettern, die Bäume
Schlauer als Sonne und Erde zusammen

ZURÜCK, ZURÜCK >
Benutzername: Farmerdave@juno.com
Paßwort: js##injunjoe6y6*l20

Irgendeinem Yankee-Traum in die Augen starrend
Zischt Farmer Dave an dem Wolkenkratzer vorbei
Fräulein Präsident folgt in Kürze, über diverse Porno-Links stolpernd
Bevor sie die Treppen zur U-Bahn hinuntersteigt

Später am selben Abend ...
Fräulein Präsident bringt die Schnittstelle an ihrem Bettsims an
Sie streichelt die Firmenzeichen und seufzt
Ein Alptraumlächeln geht langsam im Portal ihres Mundes auf

Während Fräulein Präsident schläft
Beugen sich die Maschinen des Schreckens unter den arabischen Himmel

Montag, 22. Juni 2004
Farmer Dave ist auf der Durchfahrt ... Wir empfangen Fragen aus seinem mobilen Büro
C:\TERRORISM\anthrax.doc

Im gewöhnlichen Alltag
Bewohnt Farmer Dave ein haariges Haus mit Wänden aus Gelee
Wo eine telepathische Drohne aus dem analen Hahn tropft

Eine Ärztehand, die sich im Flur windet, flößt Dave Furcht ein
(Wir sind viel größer als Dave)

Google-Suche: Magisches Amerika Bagelherz
Suchergebnisse (1-10, ansteigend)
3. Magisches Amerika GmbH führt einen Bagelherz-Anschluß ein

*** Teil 2 ***

Häuptling Bagelherz latscht zwischen seinen beiden Gemahlinnen (Schwestern) her
Er ist mittelgroß, breitschultrig und hat eine tiefe Brust
Eine Bagel-Halskette um seine Titten gebunden
Er spricht ganz offen mit seinem Arzt

Fräulein Präsident betritt den Wigwam durch den Seiteneingang
Bagelherz rollt in einem Krankenhausbett vorbei
Farmer Dave schielt aus seinem Rektum über den Operationstisch
Dr. Amerika führt den Skalp-Tanz auf

He, der Herr, stört es Sie, wenn ich mal Ihren Rucksack anprobiere?

Google-Suche: Fräulein Präsident nackt
Ergebnisse (5-10)
7. Fräulein Präsident Fickbildchen – Seemannsknochen, die durch den Hafen wirbeln
Bild 1, Bild 2, Bild 3, Bild 4 usw. …
8. Bagelherz Stammbaum – Fräulein Präsident > Zeugte jüdischen Präsidenten > Zeugte Niggerfrau usw. …

Ich wende mich dem guten Häuptling zu und frage, was ihn denn plagt
»Prostatitis,« antwortet er, »wo eigentlich meine Prostata sein sollte, habe ich eine kleine Kartoffel.«
Er spricht ganz offen mit mir
»Meine Hände mußten als erstes weg …«
»Die gute Nachricht«, kichert er, »ist, daß ich sterben werde.«

Donnerstag, 24. Juni
Nächsten Vormittag versende ich 3 Anthrax-Briefe
Ich fange an, Bio-Terrorismus als einen Akt der Reinigung zu betrachten
(Wie alle Männer bin ich ein bißchen ein Jackson Pollock im Bett)

»Zwei Cent Belohnung für die Ergreifung und Auslieferung Farmer Daves«

Der begabte Arzt besitzt eine urbane Adresse
Neben Erbrechern und dreiköpfigen Milliardären
Die Straße hinunter versteinert ein Hügel aus Kriegern
Ein feiger Terrorist hat ihnen die Glieder abgeschlagen

Drei Blocks nach Osten …
Römische Wachtposten jagen herumtollenden Bauernmädchen im Park hinterher
Während bisexuelle Touristen unter einem Baldachin aus Totempfählen schlendern
Ich folge ihnen bis zum Großen Kanal hinunter und heirate sie

Mami und ich fahren zu meiner Tubastunde
Fräulein Präsident unterrichtet Tuba in ihrer Garage
(die mit allerhand Schrott vollgestopft ist)

Jetzt bin ich in meiner Tubastunde
Michael Jackson fragt, ob er meinen Rucksack anprobieren könne … *durchaus!*
Er sagt, er werde eine Schatztruhe vergraben
die mit seinen eigenen Goldenen Schallplatten gefüllt ist
… kann ich helfen, den Graben auszuheben?

Michael Jordan trägt Hanes
Aber was für Unterhosen trägt Jacko heutzutage?
(Fräulein Präsident wirkt allerdings abgelenkt)

Farmer Dave war ein weniger bekannter College-Basketball-Trainer
Bevor er dabei erwischt wurde, in Michael Jordans Trophäenkabinett Bestechungsgelder entgegenzunehmen
Vor Michael J. Fox versohlte er mir den Hintern

Wie würdest DU dich fühlen, wenn der König des Pop gerade zerbröselte?

Ich habe zu diesem Kerl aufgeschaut …
Ich schäme mich so
Zum ersten Mal in meinem Leben habe ich über Selbstmord nachgedacht

*** Teil 3 ***

Da ist ein zerfleddertes Päckchen von Farmer Dave
Es liegt noch immer auf dem Sims, neben den Briefen und Zahlen vom letzten Jahr
(Ich könnte nicht aushalten, es zu öffnen)
Alle Gedanken wenden sich meinem Lamm zu …
Sie wäre verdrossen, wenn sie mich und Fräulein Präsident zusammen sehen würde
Sie ist eine perfekte Amerikanerin

Ich sehe Bagelherz durch Internet-Perspektiven waten
Meereswogen durch militärische Dekodiergeräte jagen
Er greift nach der Sonne, verwegen nackt und ungeschützt
Warum sollte es so sein, daß reiche Sprößlinge ihn dafür bezahlen, sich selbst zu kastrieren?

Adam Green Magazin: Ausgabe #4c
1. Saddam Hussein: Hollywood-Diktator
Meine Hand auf seinen getragenen Sneakers
Mein Herz, seine zerrissenen Hosen beklagend
2. Ein erotischer Minimoment:
Strauchelnd zwischen den nächtlichen Wänden
Stürzte ich vor einer Höhle aus Licht

In Bagelherz' gegerbte Kombüse gekuschelt
Mischt sich Farmer Dave unter die Bakterien
»Hier drin gibt's genug Sperma, um eine behelfsmäßige Geschlechtskrankheit auszubrüten«
Es gibt eine neue Region!

Fräulein Präsident kommt mit einem großen Problem zu mir …
Ich schüttele meine Zangen und starre in das Labyrinth ihrer Vagina
Binnen Sekunden lege ich eine Quelle nicht näher bezeichneter Tränen frei
Und dic Diamanten des Heiligen Thomas
Und einen jungen Farmer Dave

Überleitung:

1. Gelbe Schilfrohre als Seitentüren auf dem lustigen blauen indianischen Rad
2. In jener Nacht träumte ich, Mike Tyson wollte mich ficken
3. Am nächsten Morgen kriegte ich raus, wie man verschnörkelte Briefe schreibt
4. Ich fühlte mich besonders und zu meiner eigenen Empfindsamkeit berechtigt
5. Er hat eine Barriere zwischen sich und seinem Tonbandgerät niedergerissen
6. Verzweifelt nach einer passenden Ablenkung suchen
7. Ein Mann braucht einen Kalender, um fahrplanmäßig zu masturbieren
8. Computerspielschnittstelle …
(Videospielpatroneninnereien)

9. Geruch von Radiergummis und getrocknetem
Speichel auf Schwanz
10. »An umgebendem Raum läßt sich nicht nuckeln«
11. Schlangenaugen rote Punkte wie Smarties
12. Tiere sind die kostbarsten Juwelen
13. Ich schwärmte nicht unbedingt von der Freundlichkeit in ihren Augen
14. Hölzerne Brötchen (Vaginas)
15. Ich stimme mit etwa 50% deiner Waschzettel überein
16. Mein Rucksack ist das Portal
17. »Frauen sind im Grunde großartig … bis sie anfangen, sich zu bewegen«
18. »Menschen sind im Grunde gut … außer ich bin unterkühlt«

Jetzt rein in den gigantischen Golfball in Disney World …

Michael Jackson und ich haben beschlossen,
bei Kellogg's Diner zu speisen
Heute nacht sind die Buden liebesapfelrot
Der Tunnel der Liebe ist eine Passage durch
Michael Jacksons Augen
Sie will nicht, daß ihre Liebe wie meine aussieht

Ich präsentiere George Lucas als den Zauberer von Oz
Er lauert hinter einem Vorhang, der aus dem Gewebe
der Unterhaltung besteht
Entflohene Gefangene heben Gräben aus im Zitronensonnenuntergang
Ihre leeren Taschen durchfeuchtet von heißem
menschlichem Blut

Kaputte abartige Krankheit
In Stücke zerschnitten und den Hügel runtergerollt
Aber die Krankheit hört trotzdem nicht auf, sich zum
Ausdruck zu bringen

Judenpräsident fährt neben uns in einem
schicken Wagen vor
Häuptling Bagelherz und Fräulein Präsident klettern an
Bord des Wagens
Und kehren ins Lager zurück

*** Teil 4 ***

Dr. Amerika sitzt einfach da und glotzt
»Normalerweise bringen wir Schmerzen nicht mit
so etwas in Zusammenhang ...«
Ich sah die Goldbarren hinter dem Berg aufsteigen
Ich binde meine Liebe im Blut des Stinktiers

Letztes Jahr zähmten wir eine wilde Nutte
Und schlossen eine umfassende Studie über Heroismus ab
Dieses Jahr posieren wir als ein ägyptischer Rockstar
Auf der Times Square-Ausstellung

Bagelherz, so krank wie es seine Angewohnheiten
klarmachen werden
Kauert hinter dem Gehsteigverkäufer, fingert an seiner
Bagel-Halskette rum
Detektive suchen die Trümmer nach entflohenen
Gefangenen ab
Prunk, Stadtstreicher, geistlose Lügen!

In der Zwischenzeit schlage ich vor, daß du dich
mit deinem Ex-Freund aussöhnst
Ich liebe seinen Mount Kisco-Akzent

Der Staub von Regenbögen hagelt auf die 9th Street
nieder
Ein summendes Geräusch erfüllt das Badezimmer
Abgeschnittene Haare sammeln sich auf dem gefliesten
Boden an

Dr. Amerika durchblättert seine Briefmarkensammlung
Zwischen Klienten wärmt Fräulein Präsident einen Topf
Bauernsuppe auf
Ich kenne dieses Geräusch … es ist das Geräusch der
Erwartung
Sie wird gleich mit meinem Hochzeitsgeschenk nach
Hause kommen

Bagelherz liegt rücklings auf dem Operationstisch
Bungee-Bänder stecken in seiner wildbretartigen Kehle,
Tränen fließen sein Gesicht hinab
Ein blasser Orgasmus braut sich in seinen Eingeweiden
zusammen
Ich löse ihn von den Eisenbahnschienen und pflanze ihn
in meinen persönlichen Privatgarten

Ich versuche, mein Lächeln beizubehalten, während
mein Auto in der Werkstatt ist
Allah, mach, daß die Gefühlswellen in Melodien
übergehen
Bauernmädchen!

Wer gebar einen Wurf farbiger Wunder!
Wer wurde im intellektuellen Diskurs trainiert!
Wer blutet mit Zärtlichkeit auf meine Seele, die wie eine leere Glühbirnenfassung ist!
Ein genesender Neger!
Es ist, als sei man der Kapitän eines Schiffs, das niemals Land erreicht
Und wir versuchen, die Bedeutung des Sports zu vergessen

Sie besteht auf einer strikten Erbschaft
Voller Scham über die Sklaverei
Und all jene mit positivem Testergebnis in Obszönität
Fräulein Präsident schmeißt einen Speer nach mir

Dermaßen in Verlegenheit gebracht durch die Ungerechtigkeit!
Solch hysterisches Weinen!
Sie spannt meinen Kopf in Position ...
Um den reichen Jungen lächeln zu sehen
Während mein Vater unter dem Tisch gekreuzigt wird
Fliehe ich mit Kind zum Schrein von Hollywood

Voller Scham über Gästelisten und Testikel
In Verlegenheit gebracht durch Zärtlichkeit und Scham
Voller Scham über Worte und Krankheiten
Voller Scham über Verlegenheit und die Insignien der Leiden ...

Speere regnen auf die 9th Street nieder
Spießen die heiligen Hippies von Manhattan auf

Energie rinnt in die Erde
Wo sind die majestätischen Götter der grenzenlosen
magischen Freiheit?
Frage: Wo sind all die Damen hin?
Antwort: Fluchen und für Trinkgeld arbeiten
Der Aufgeiler grapscht meinen Schwanz und zerrt daran

Jauchzend zu der Musik seines heiligen Herz-Liedes
Treibt Farmer Dave einen Speer in Fräulein Präsident
Die Trommeln des Umstands, schlagt sie mit aller Kraft
Das Spektrum des Urteils wird durch Träume von einer
Belohnung verdunkelt

Wir reiten auf den Kauwerkzeugen eines nuklearen
Zyklopen
Unser Körper ist eine komplex strukturierte Gesellschaft
Verraten durch eine gewaltige Energiewelle
Unsere U-Bahn-Gebete, von Meistern der Schwarzen
Magie unterwandert
Fräulein Präsident, Sie sollten sich stellen

Die Hand in der Kamera bildet jetzt eine wütende Faust
Verraten durch leere Vergnügungen und falsche Paarung!
Verraten durch Nervenschädigung und hoffnungsloses
Licht!

Rotkehlhüttensänger bis zur Verrücktheit geschüttelt
in einem violetten Wirbelwind
An der Taille ermordet und Lehm heraushustend
Wir beten um herabstoßende Engelsarme, die uns
herausholen
Wir beten um die Hand außerhalb der Maschine …

*** Teil 5 ***

Schneide, mein Freund, Erzähl keine Lüge
Sieh zu, wie ich sage, mein Freund ist Spion

Es ist 1986
Ich bin 5 Jahre alt – es ist der erste Kindergartentag
Jesse Tisch sitzt neben mir, baut was mit Klötzen
Wir versuchen, den Eiffelturm zu konstruieren
(Damals habe ich nur selten konstruktive Kritik zu
schätzen gewußt)
Schhh … das Hundekruzifix schläft
Krabbe krabbelt Bein hoch, erreicht die Schamsonne
Der Ausdruck persönlicher Vorliebe ist unser Sport

Nimm meine Frau zum Beispiel
Eine total disziplinierte Mieze
Sie kommt jede Nacht nach Hause (mehr oder weniger)
Und massiert stets meine Breitseite, bevor wir
zu Bett gehen …
Zersplitterte hölzerne Geheimnisse lauern in den Blasen
Korallenbänder kentern durch die Lasercode-Lesegeräte
Anmerkung: Man benötigt einen Codeleser, um ein Spiel
zu entblättern
Und die Maschinerie darunter aufzudecken
Wer auch immer das Spiel verkauft, erhält das meiste
Geld und den *ersten* Lacher

Wohin auch immer ich gehe, trage ich stets eine
Hemisphäre der Scham mit mir herum
Andauernd vibriert eine Stimme hinter dem Vorhang

Und ich arbeite mit einem toten Herz
Ich wende mich ab, als die Maschine eine freundliche
Dame niedertrampelt

Die Landschaften eines Orkangedächtnisses sind ihren
Besitzern heilig
Ich sah die goldenen Stäbe hinter dem Berg aufsteigen
Die Strahlen versanken in meiner Haut wie Fischhaken
Zogen mich an das Licht, das ich vergessen hatte
Ich konnte kein Licht mehr halten

Ich trage ein kleines Stück Eisenkies bei mir
Von weither, aus der Schatztruhe im Himmel
Meine Last treibt mich unter die Erde
Wo ich ihre Insignien nur kurze Zeit genießen kann …
Bis ich weniger habe als ich wollen könnte

Hinter einer Kiste mit anonymen Körperteilen
Sehe ich Blumenkinder über die Hänge fegen
Ihr Hasenzahnlächeln delirierend vor Hoffnung

Meine größte Angst ist es, mit den Schlüsseln in der
Hand zu sterben
Brot macht Butter … es ist die Wissenschaft vom Glauben
Vielleicht wird ein Gummiband irgendwie auftauchen
Mein Lamm ruft mich nach Hause

Fertiggestellt am 3. Juli 2004

Abbildungsnachweise

Seite 9 Foto von Phil Knott
Seite 17 Foto von Jaiko Suzuki
Seite 35 Foto von Amanda DeCadanet
Seite 51 Illustration von Adam Green

Diskographie

mit Kimya Dawson:
The Moldy Peaches: The Moldy Peaches. Rough Trade 2000.
The Moldy Peaches: Who's Got The Crack? Rough Trade 2001
The Moldy Peaches: Country Fair/Rainbows. Rough Trade 2002
The Moldy Peaches: Unreleased Cutz and Live Jamz 1994-2002. Rough Trade 2002.

Various Artists: Antifolk Compilation Vol. 1. Rough Trade 2002.

Adam Green: Dance With Me. Rough Trade 2002. (Maxi)
Adam Green: Garfield. Rough Trade 2002.
Adam Green: Friends Of Mine. Rough Trade 2003.
Adam Green: Jessica/Kokomo. Rough Trade 2003. (Maxi)
Adam Green: Friends Of Mine. Rough Trade 2004. (Maxi)
Adam Green: Gemstones. Rough Trade 2005
Adam Green: Emily. Rough Trade 2005. (Maxi)

www.adamgreen.net

Thomas Meinecke

The Church of John F. Kennedy

Roman
edition suhrkamp 1997
245 Seiten

»Eines der intelligentesten und sprachlich reizvollsten Bücher des Jahres«, schrieb die *Badische Zeitung* über Thomas Meineckes 1996 erschienenen Roman *The Church of John F. Kennedy*. Die *Frankfurter Rundschau* verglich den Roman mit dem *Steinernen Herz* von Arno Schmidt. Er sei »eine traumwandlerisch gelungene Anknüpfung an ein fast schon vergessenes Meisterwerk der 50er Jahre«.
In seinem literarischen Roadmovie macht sich Meinecke auf die Suche nach deutschen Spuren in Amerika Anfang der 90er Jahre.
Dem Reisenden Wenzel Assmann bewahrheitet sich die These, daß die USA zwar imstande sind, die ganze Welt über den Einheitskamm ihres »Way of Life« zu scheren, daß sie nach innen jedoch eine bis heute äußerst heterogene Kulturlandschaft voller weißer Flecken und schwarzer Löcher aufweisen.

NF 328/1/2.01

Andreas Neumeister

Gut laut

Roman
Gebunden. 184 Seiten
suhrkamp taschenbuch 3282. 192 Seiten

»Es gibt Leute, in deren Leben spielt Musik eine völlig nebensächliche Rolle, er kenne Leute, die hören nicht mal Klassik. Er kenne Menschen, in Mjunik lebende Menschen, sagt Roman, die sich in dieser musikbesessenen Epoche weder für Popmusik noch für irgendeine andere Art von Musik interessieren. Seltsam, sagt Roman, Zeitgenossen, scheinbare Zeitgenossen, die bei dem Wort Kraftwerk einfach nur an banale Stromerzeugung denken, machen ihn krank.«
Andreas Neumeister folgt in seinem furiosen Prosamonolog dem elektronischen Rhythmus des »Ebenjetzt«, verliert dabei aber nicht aus dem Blick, daß das rasende »Musikbesessenheitszeitalter« eine Geschichte hat: Mit dem großartigen Stadiondach für die Olympischen Spiele 1972, dem ersten Kassettenrecorder, spätestens mit Donna Summer und Giorgio Moroder's Late-Seventies Plastic Sound of Munich endet für ihn die Nachkriegsära, beginnt die überfällige Unterminierung »dieses Katastrophenjahrhunderts« und die trotzige Vorwegnahme des neuen Jahrtausends.

NF 326/1/2.01